# No Time to Save

*Lewis Davies*

*Lewis Davies*

For my buddies
Jamie & Gill
-x-

Fay

*Lewis Davies*

# The Chapters

*Lewis Davies*

# The Prologue

Most stories that I have read are written based on experiences and influences that the author, at some point or another, has drawn from various sources.

A story about fact, a story about love, about a childhood or an event. They have a message to portray or a subliminal guide to life. A pathway to enlightenment reflecting what everyone in their hearts truly desires. An answer to the many challenges that face us in our daily struggle with reality or an escape from it.

However, this story is none of these. It is just a story of a boy, plain and simple. A story of a boy, who goes to school, eats his greens, plays rugby with his friends and is obsessed with a girl in his class.

But this story, however pointless the reader may find it to begin with, should be persevered and some enjoyment may come from reading it.

*Lewis Davies*

Too much time is spent these days trying to solve the world's problems through literature. This story began as a short tale for personal amusement. It had no direction and as it progressed and the short story turned into a longer story it still had no direction. When the story was eventually wrapped up several months after its beginning, several pages after its intention, it seemed that as the last word was typed, the tale finally seemed to know where it was going.

Many hours were spent wondering where the next word would come from, so on pure imagination and sheer determination to achieve what others find so easy, the story was finally completed.

The art of writing a book has not been looked at in the compiling of this story. It is as raw as it was when it entered the author's head. So, if the reader is looking for a tale written with perfect grammar, punctuation, and text, then you should not bother to read beyond this point.

However, if the reader does not mind the odd spelling mistake here and there or the text rolling along, taking your imagination off in different directions, then please read on.

*The Author*

*Lewis Davies*

"There are really four dimensions, three which we call the three planes of Space, and a fourth, Time." *H.G. Wells*

*Lewis Davies*

# Chapter I

## *The Quarry*

It began on a Wednesday at 8.30am. Charlie Davies was roused from a deep sleep by his alarm clock. As Darth Vader announced, "The force is strong with this one," Charlie climbed out of bed, got dressed and headed downstairs to the kitchen.

It was the summer holidays and although his mum had already gone to work, Charlie had the whole day to himself. It would be the last summer before starting a new adventure. Charlie had excelled in his final exams and was looking forward to beginning a 3-year degree in Environmental Sciences at University.

Mulling over his cereal on whether to play his computer games all day or go out and enjoy the summer sun, Charlie decided the weather was too good to miss.

It was the first day since the start of the holidays, a week ago, that the weather had turned for the better. Severe rain had lashed the east coast for a fortnight causing damage to many villages in the area.

His mind made up, Charlie slipped on his trainers, grabbed his binoculars and a chocolate bar for later and made a beeline for the door.

Hopping over the back gate into the woodland beyond, Charlie shrugged off the claustrophobia of the last weak and breathed in the air. A smile of anticipation came to his face and as Charlie wandered further into the wood, he wondered what the day would bring.

Chaffinches flitted through the trees and a woodpecker drummed in the distance. As Charlie walked, a vole quickly scurried out of his way.

∞

The path he was following eventually joined a tarmac cycle track that used to be an old railway line. Charlie turned left and followed it for 10 minutes then turned off down a steep embankment to the street where his friend, Jamie Young, lived.

Jamie was still in bed and it took several bangs on the letterbox to have him finally open the door to Charlie.

"You lazy sod!" Charlie said as Jamie blearily gave him the evil eye. "The weather is fab. Come on, put some clothes on and drag your fat ass out here".

"I'll need a coffee first," muttered Jamie, "then we'll go. Oh, and I resent the fat ass remark," he said with a half-smile.

∞

*Lewis Davies*

Half an hour later, the two boys were heading through the village high street towards the river.

"I'm telling ya, she said that she thought you were funny."

"Funny ha-ha or funny weird?" replied Charlie to his friend's statement.

"Funny ha-ha probably," said Jamie, "It doesn't really matter; the thing is she knows your name and who you are."

"Whatever," said Charlie, "I'm not fussed. It doesn't bother me whether she does or not."

"Bollocks, you do so!" replied Jamie rather loudly. "You've fancied the pants off Hannah since second year, ever since the Christmas dance where you ate so much you puked all over the dance floor!"

"That was four years ago and it was you that puked," said Charlie in a weary voice.

∞

Their walking had carried them along the riverbank west and around to the north. The river had burst its banks three days previous but, due to the sandy soil of the area, the levels had receded back to normal leaving the ground soft underfoot.

Man-made debris joined the many broken branches that made up the flotsam left over from the storm. The brown water carried it downstream faster than the boys walked. It was 9.30am and the morning sun was heating up the land, causing a low blanket of mist to evaporate around the boys' feet.

A moorhen battled through the usually calm current while sedge and reed warblers sang in the rushes that lined the banks. Swallows and martins dipped across the water, picking off insects.

As the river curved north, the boys turned left along a track created by cattle. The track was muddy and churned up so they had to carefully pick their way along the dips and troughs full of rainwater.

Jamie and Charlie knew where they were heading to, as the track ended at a gate. Through it they entered another field that seemed to have been left to nature, a wide-open piece of land with long grasses, thistles and sedges. The field sloped down at a steady angle towards a sheer drop and as the boys descended, grasshoppers and diurnal moths hopped and flew out of their path.

∞

Eventually they arrived at their destination at the bottom of the field.

Two decades ago, the local villages acquired all their building materials from the local sandstone quarry whose cliffs the boys now stood on.

Abandoned after the excavation contract expired, the quarry was now home to burnt-out cars, broken beer bottles and the occasional trail biker.

However, the boys were here for one thing.

For the past two years, a pair of peregrine falcon had been nesting in the quarry and Charlie knew that that year the birds had raised two young. As they weaved their way down into the quarry, the boys flushed a small flock of feral pigeon from the cliff. Suddenly, a movement caught the boy's eye and a falcon plummeted through the birds catching one of the pigeons on its wing, sending the bird tumbling to the floor below. Instantly the bird of prey was on its victim, grabbing its prey at the neck and twisting.

As Charlie watched through his binoculars, the pigeon struggled less and less, then lay still.

∞

# Chapter II

## *The Blackness*

"Bloody Hell!" exclaimed Jamie, "That was awesome!"

Charlie said nothing. He was entranced by the predator now pulling feathers from the dead bird in its talons. Charlie had seen the parents catch prey before but he had never seen a young bird hunt. It was incredible to think that two months ago the falcon before him was just a ball of fluff in its nest on the quarry face. Now it was an elite killing machine.

"Now you know why I like birds!" said Charlie.

"But not Hannah Wilson though, eh?" teased Jamie.

Charlie ignored him as the two continued their decent into the quarry. As they approached the falcon it looked up at them and immediately took off with its kill, flying over their heads and disappearing over the lip of the quarry.

The torrential rain had caused several landslides in the quarry. In places the boys had to pick their way over large piles of boulders and sand.

Here and there, the ground had given way to create deep depressions and cracks, giving the impression of being on the moon.

"So, what are you gonna do about Hannah?" asked Jamie.

Charlie, deep in thought, decided to put his friends mind at rest.

"When we get back to school I'll talk to her, alright?" he said. "I do like her and I'll try my luck. If she says no then at least I know where I stand."

"Fair enough," said Jamie, "but if she says no can I have a shot?" Charlie's face said it all and Jamie responded with a pat on the back. "Just kidding," he said, "I don't even like blondes!"

∞

The boys continued further down into the quarry, descending to the next level. The ground was softer than the ridge they had just come along and, from time to time, the boys found their feet sinking in to the sand.

"This is getting ridiculous," shouted Jamie, "where the bloody hell are you taking us?"

"To that wooded spot up on the other side," Charlie said. "You know. Where we threw that huge boulder down the hill last year on to that burnt out Escort? There's a buzzard nest nearby."

"Bloody birds!" mumbled Jamie. "These are my good trainers."

The two of them continued to make their way across the quarry. Charlie was in front when suddenly Jamie screamed. As Charlie spun around, he laughed aloud. Jamie was on his left knee with his right leg completely embedded in the ground, up to his groin.

Charlie quickly rushed over and helped his friend out of his prison.

"What happened there? Are you alright?" Charlie asked.

"Yeah, I'm fine," Jamie spat, "apart from the bloody sand in my shoes!" He brushed himself down, sat on a rock, took out his Zippo and lit a cigarette. "That scared the shit out of me!"

"This ground isn't stable, there's too much water in the soil," said Charlie.

"I *noticed* that," said Jamie sarcastically exhaling deeply. "It felt like there was nothing underneath my foot." He finished his cigarette and very carefully stubbed it out on the ground.

"OK, we'll have to go carefully over to that next ridge there." Charlie pointed a hundred meters in front of them. "We should be fine once we get to the rocks."

They set off again, but this time not so boldly. Testing the ground every step, the boys edged closer to the safety of the ridge.

∞

The sun was high now and both boys were sweating through the effort of their journey. A heat haze rippled above the ground and the birds were quiet.

They were carefully edging their way across the baking quarry when they became aware of a low rumbling. They were used to aircraft from the nearby RAF base passing overhead but this was unlike any sound they had heard before.

It began as a deep low growl, just audible, and began to get louder as if the sound was approaching.

The boys stopped, looking not to the sky but to the ground. The sound *was* approaching but not from the air, from below!

"What the hell is that?" asked Jamie.

"Not a clue but I think we'd better move a bit quicker," replied Charlie, a little nervous.

They began to jog, stumbling every few meters as the loose sand began to give way.

Charlie's heart was pounding. He was scared and knew that Jamie was too. The rumbling grew until they could not hear their own breaths, full of confusion. The noise was deafening and echoed off the quarry walls. "Just a few more meters," thought Charlie. He could now see the surface of the ground vibrating as the stones and pebbles around them began to disappear below the earth.

"Run!" shouted Jamie. Charlie did not need to be told twice and dived towards the rocky ridge. The ground continued to give way under every step and the rumbling was beginning to hurt their ears.

Charlie could see the ridge getting closer and knew they were going to make it. With relief on his face he stumbled on with a new energy. His legs were sinking with every step now and it felt as if he was wading through water.

Suddenly his foot hit ground beneath that did not shift under his weight. The ridge was now only 6 meters away and as Charlie lifted his other leg he turned and smiled back at Jamie.

Jamie wasn't there! There was nothing but the ground Charlie had just waded across. Charlie stared at the blank, shifting sand and panic rose in his throat as he began to see the quarry walls around him rise. It took him a split second to realise it was him that was sinking. The ground was giving way!

He was already up to his knees in sand and when Charlie managed to free one leg his other one sank deeper. Before he knew it, he was up to his waist. He tried to pull himself up but his hands and arms sank into the loose earth.

As he sank further down, he let out a terrified scream for help. Sand and dirt filled his mouth. The noise of the rumbling softened as sand filled his ears. Charlie closed his eyes as the earth swallowed him. His lungs beginning to contract as the remaining pockets of air disappeared.

The last thing Charlie felt before unconsciousness overwhelmed him... was nothing.

∞

# Chapter III

## *The Body*

The freezing water began to fill his lungs as Charlie tried to gasp for air. Kicking with what little strength he had, he finally broke the surface. Coughing up the last of the water in his airways his chest filled with sweet, sweet oxygen.

Disorientated, Charlie tried to remember how he came to be floating along in an ice-cold river. Well, he assumed it was a river.

It was pitch black and he had no sense of direction or size. The current carried him onwards and although he tried, Charlie could not feel any banks on either side.

As his breathing steadied, he became aware that his mouth was full of sand. As he took a mouth full of water to rinse it out, Charlie suddenly remembered it all: the quarry, the noise, the sand - Jamie.

Where was his friend? Where was he? Charlie began to panic again as the reality dawned on him and the low temperature of the water began to cool his blood.

His breathing came in short bursts. Unable to keep his head above water any longer, Charlie finally succumbed to the inevitable. He slowly sank below the surface as the current carried him on through the darkness.

*Lewis Davies*

Suddenly his feet scraped something hard, the bottom of the river!

He kicked off from it and resurfaced, gasping. The current was beginning to slow and as Charlie looked through stinging eyes toward the direction he was moving, a faint light began to grow. He could make out dark walls of rock all around him. The river was passing through a vast cavern. As he stared, Charlie saw the light getting brighter and brighter until a wall of light some twelve meters across and eight meters high was clearly visible up ahead. The walls of the cavern on either side began to close in, as if tapering to the point of light.

The flow of the water slowed even more and Charlie felt his feet beginning to drag on the ground below the surface. As he was carried closer to the wall of light, Charlie could maintain his balance and wade as the water level dropped.

Only up to his knees, the water was a gentle stream when Charlie began to make out the line of land up ahead. As he approached, he saw that it was a small beach, illuminated at the base of the wall as if on a moonlit night.

Charlie was still some fifteen meters away when he realised something lay on the beach. With a dawn of realisation, he began to splash through the stream, now only ankle deep.

Finally, he collapsed next to the shape he saw lying motionless. Tearfully Charlie rolled the body over to stare into the lifeless eyes of his friend.

*Lewis Davies*

∞

Charlie lay there with Jamie in his arms for a lifetime, it seemed. Lost, scared and alone, he stared vacantly at the wall of light until his eyes stung. The only rational explanation for the brightness had to be algae. Charlie had read that some plants give off a luminescent glow through a biological reaction. He was ashamed that he was trying to work this out while his friend lay dead in his arms. Where was his compassion, his remorse?

Charlie gave in to his grief and wept again.

∞

He awoke with a start from a strange dream involving figures dressed in white. But just as soon as he tried to remember it, the dream slipped back into his sub-consciousness.

Charlie was shivering. The cold had turned his lips blue and his body ached with the effort of trying to stay warm. How long had he been unconscious?

The first thing he noticed was the light emanating from the wall behind him had dimmed. As his eyes became accustomed to the darkness, he realised that it was only coming from one part of the cavern.

Slowly getting to his feet, he began to work his way over to the light's source. Standing in front of the wall, Charlie began to run his hands over it, feeling for any part that he could maybe break off and use as a torch. But there were no handholds, grooves or rough texture to the rock - it was smooth like a plate of glass. And the glow was coming from inside the wall!

Confused, he began to feel his way along, until he felt the rough, coldness of the natural rock to the left, then to the right.

Completely barren of any markings, it looked as though the glassy surface continued the same up to the roof of the cavern, some 8 meters up.

So preoccupied was he with the wall, Charlie had forgotten about Jamie still lying motionless beside the water. He wearily turned around. His whole body, physically and emotionally drained, was on the verge of collapse.

What could he do now? With no idea of where he was or where to go and inconsolable about his lifeless friend, Charlie began to cry again.

But as he approached the spot where Jamie had lain, the low light illuminated bare ground. The impressions in the sand where they had been lying were clear to see, but Jamie's body had gone. Panicking, Charlie rushed back into the cold water thinking that maybe his friend had been washed back in, but he could find no trace.

Charlie was certain that Jamie had still been there when he got up to investigate the wall, but the more he tried to remember, the more he doubted himself.

"Maybe Jamie wasn't there when I woke up?" he thought. His mind raced with confusion. He had never felt more alone.

∞

# Chapter IV

## *The Wall*

He sat on the shore for what seemed like hours, staring into the water while tears smeared the dirt on his cheeks.

An eternity passed until Charlie, seeming to reach a decision, picked himself back up and stood, once again facing the wall of light.

In sheer frustration, Charlie snatched a loose rock from the ground, stood back and hurled it at the glassy surface. As it struck it launched a shower of sparks, silent but dazzlingly bright. The rock disappeared but no debris or dust fell. The light had engulfed it as if the wall had swallowed the missile in its entirety.

Charlie had expected the wall to shatter like glass and his heart leapt when it did not. Unable to fathom what had just happened, he reached for another stone and threw it at the wall. The same thing happened again. The stone passed through without a scar and disappeared.

Although he could not shake the image of his dead friend from his head, Charlie knew that if he were to survive, he would have to try and leave this unforgiving cave.

He felt the wall again, solid as before with no handholds, cracks or grooves. He tried punching his hand through it, but ended up bruising his knuckles. The wall stayed unyielding and once again Charlie felt his confidence leaving him. He launched another stone. Yet again it vanished through the wall.

After trying to punch his way through a third time, Charlie collapsed on the sand, nursing his bleeding knuckles.

It was hopeless. He could not understand why the stones passed through and he could not. Was he too big? Was there a way through, or was it really a solid wall?

Then it dawned on him. Maybe he was not going fast enough. If he were wrong, it would be like running full steam into concrete. If he was right, would he be able to pass right through or would he be trapped forever within the wall?

Charlie resolved himself to at least attempt it. With no other options, and determined not to be trapped in the cave until the inevitable, Charlie walked back into the freezing watery shallows giving himself as much of a run up as he could.

Focused on his target, he let his muscles relax and, ignoring the panic and fear surging through his whole being, began to run. Jamie's face again flashed in his mind and as he raced on closer to the wall, tears began to well up Charlie's eyes again.

"I am so sorry Jamie!" he cried. As the wall loomed up, Charlie raised his hands in front of him to take the full force of the impact that would surely come.

Closing his eyes instinctively, he felt a sharp pain, not in his arms as they hit the wall, but all through his body like an electric charge had coursed through every pore.

Charlie stumbled in shock, dropped to his knees and came to a halt on his front, his face pressed against the ground.

The pain subsided as quickly as it came, but fearing what he might see,

Charlie kept his eyes closed. He tried to lift a finger off the cold, smooth surface he lay on and found that he could easily. Cautiously, he slowly opened one eye. He quickly closed it again as the searing light pierced his retina.

After a few minutes, he carefully allowed light to leak under his eyelids. Charlie was relieved that the brightness has subsided and he could open his eyes fully, taking in his surroundings.

The first thing he noticed was the wall opposite him. It was made of stone, but not rough, natural rock like the cave. This stone was smooth with no texture and no edges. Where it met the floor, it curved down horizontally. His eyes followed it as it went underneath him. Turning his head, he saw it continue to the right, curving up the opposite wall and over his head on a continuous arc.

Charlie lifted his head and stared out in front of him. He was lying in a corridor that stretched off into the darkness. The light source came from behind him and as he turned around, he saw the familiar glowing wall barring his way back. He slowly clambered to his feet and ran his hands over the smooth glass-like surface. It was as solid as before. Looking along the floor, behind him he found one of the stones he had thrown earlier. Once again, he hurled it at the wall and, as before, it disappeared in a blinding shower of sparks. Then, nothing.

With no desire to attempt to return the cave where only the freezing cold water awaited him, Charlie turned and looked down the corridor. The air was still, odourless but seemed warmer than in the cavern and he could feel the chill beginning to leave his body.

*Lewis Davies*

With no other choice but to venture forward, Charlie began to edge slowly down the darkening passageway.

∞

# Chapter V

## *The Tunnel*

Keeping close to the left sidewall by running his hand along it, Charlie's heart began to beat loudly in the silent darkness that closed around him. After a few minutes, he was plunged into impenetrable blackness as the last of the light behind finally left him. Charlie began to use two hands to find his way and that was how he discovered the wall change texture from a stone surface to a metallic like feel. Every so often, Charlie's fingers ran over a small raise in the wall that gave the impression of rivets or nails embedded in the cold surface.

He longed for light to guide his way but none came. Charlie edged further along the wall, his feet shuffling carefully in case any dips or drops appeared in the floor.

Suddenly, his right hand felt an edge to the wall. It was a corner and as he slowly put his head around, Charlie felt a warm breeze coming down a new corridor leading off to the left.

Not knowing if the corridor he was in led further on and not wanting to leave the safety of the wall, Charlie made the decision to take this new path and the promise of freedom as the refreshing wind touched his face.

As before, Charlie edged carefully along the new wall heading toward the source of the breeze.

Before long, Charlie realised he was sweating. The warmth had increased and the wall was longer cold to the touch. The breeze was intensifying to and as Charlie continued forward, he began to find it difficult to stand up straight. The breeze had turned into a wind and then a gale.

Nevertheless, above the howling noise, Charlie began to hear a familiar sound. A low rumble was just audible but, unlike before, it was coming from along the tunnel.

The wind became so strong that Charlie had to drop to his knees in fear that he would be blown over. The rumbling increased and Charlie let go of the wall so he could place his hands over his ears to block out the deafening cacophony that now reverberated around the walls.

Suddenly the wind stopped, and as the noise continued, Charlie was able to stand up again. With his hands still over his ears, he made his way further down the tunnel still keeling to the wall for guidance. The rumbling began to fade and eventually subsided altogether as Charlie placed his hands back on the wall for balance. The combination of the heat and the wind had almost dried Charlie's clothes entirely and feeling invigorated, he quickened his pace down the tunnel, determined to get to the end of it all.

He had gone no more than a few feet when the end did come. A solid wall across the tunnel barred his path. Charlie traced his hands around from the wall he had followed to the new wall and then over to where it joined the opposite wall running parallel to the one Charlie had followed.

Running his hands back again, Charlie cautiously rapped his knuckles against the wall barring his way. The metallic noise echoed down the corridor like an empty casket. He tried the left wall but his knuckles only gave off a dull thud.

His heart began to quicken, Charlie pushed his shoulder against the new wall. It didn't move. He began to run his hands all over the wall trying to find an edge or handle. It was smooth.

"There has to be a way through," Charlie said aloud. "If only I had a bit of light". In frustration, he slumped down in the darkness with his back to the wall. His legs stretched out in front of him, Charlie began to think of his family; his mother, father, sister. Remorse began to well up inside when he thought of Jamie, and his family. Overwhelmed by grief again, Charlie began to cry, so he did not notice at first what his hand had been resting on for the last few minutes.

∞

# Chapter VI

## *The Chance*

It was an object, small and solid, square in shape. Suddenly Charlie realised what it was and leapt to his feet wiping the tears away.

How it got there, he did not know but Charlie hoped that Jamie's zippo lighter still worked even after being submerged in the underground river.

Charlie fumbled in the dark and eventually flipped the hinged lighter lid open. Locating the small wheel that sparks the flint, Charlie, with his hands shaking dragged his thumb down it. Nothing happened. He tried again but still nothing. The third time, however, a brief spark ignited in the darkness blinding Charlie for an instant. He tried repeatedly; the spark came but no flame.

"The wick must be damp". He sat for a while and thought of his next move. If he continued to spark the flint, it would eventually wear out. What he needed was something dry but even then, the spark from the flint would not be enough to ignite it. Then it came to him. Even if the lighter were water logged, there would be enough lighter fluid soaked into the gauze in the main part of the lighter.

Charlie carefully turned the lighter over and worked the zippo out of its casing. A strong smell of lighter fluid filled Charlie's nostrils and he smiled when he realised his plan could work.

He leant on the floor with one hand and guided his other with the gauze in it, placing it next to his positioned hand. Keeping his hand in place, Charlie then worked the lighter around in his hand so his thumb was on the ignition wheel.

Searching blindly, he felt the gauze touch the lighter. Charlie drew his thumb over the wheel again. Expecting to have to try more than once, he was taken by surprise as the spark from the flint ignited the fuel soaked gauze first time.

The corridor lit up in what Charlie felt to be the most extreme level of light he had ever seen. After the darkness he had become accustomed to, Charlie's eyes were burning. After a moment, he was relieved that, he could begin to make out his surroundings but before he could investigate further, he tore a part of the bottom of his t-shirt off and applied it to the flame. The t-shirt had become like tinder after the intenseness of the heat and wind earlier. Charlie now had more light so he turned his attention to the walls.

They were dazzling white and where Charlie had felt rivets, bright blue bulbs were embedded into the wall in parallel lines running vertical from the floor up the wall, over his head and back down.

He turned to the door and gasped. It was also white but covering it was a symmetrical red pattern stretching from the ceiling to the floor. The pattern was made of block lines branching out from each other and joining inverted pentagonal shape that was higher than Charlie was. Within the pentagon, several red circles formed a vertical line on either side of a red image glowing in the light.

The image consisted of seven shapes that looked like eyes encompassing two sets of outstretched wings overlapping. On closer inspection, it seemed as if the pairs of wings in the middle had a subtle edge to them as opposed to the smoothness of the rest of the door.

Charlie gently ran his fingers over the pattern. It felt as smooth as the rest of the door, which was why he probably missed it in the dark.

Charlie tore off another piece of t-shirt to fuel the fire behind him, which was gradually dying.

He looked at the double wings again. They definitely had an edge to them as if they were embedded in the door.

Instinct took over and as if something was willing him to do so, Charlie placed two fingers against the symbol and pushed. Not knowing what was going to happen, he jumped back behind his makeshift fire.

He did not have to. The door didn't swing out but instantly turned completely white like the surrounding walls and, vanished!

∞

# Chapter VII

## *The Meeting*

Charlie was not sure what to expect. Maybe a room or another corridor waited on the other side but, when the cool breeze touched his face and he stepped out onto the dark grass under a starlit sky, Charlie wept with relief and collapsed to his knees. The opening that he had come through returned to its solid form obscuring the fire and once again, Charlie was surrounded by darkness but this time he could just see by the light of the stars.

The doorway was a rock face, now dark, stretching up to a small ledge twenty feet above and then a huge mountain, larger than Charlie has ever seen. He knew there were no mountains in his area so, where was he?

The air was so sweet compared to the staleness in the corridor and Charlie breathed deeply as he scanned over his new surroundings. To his left and front, the grass stretched further than his eyes could see. Behind him was the mountain and to his right there was a small forest, similar to the one he had walked through to get to Jamie's house. That seemed a lifetime ago. If only he had known that just a few hours had passed since he had taken that walk and Charlie should now have been standing under a bright warm sun instead of a starlit sky.

Charlie slowly moved towards the forest, making sure he kept the rock face in sight. As he approached the first line of trees, Charlie noticed a pale green glow coming from the base of one of the trees further into the wood.    Intrigued    he moved closer until he knelt down to examine the strange light. Right on top of it, Charlie could see that it was actually a standard flip switch like you would have for a light in your home or an electric socket.

It was lit up green by a white bulb emanating through the green switch, which can only be described as being made of plastic. Such a familiar object compared to the alien environment he had recently experienced. Charlie reached over, held it between thumb and forefinger and slowly flipped the switch down from its upright position.

*Lewis Davies*

Instantly, there was a blinding flash, the world lit up and stayed. The forest that Charlie was in, the surrounding grass, mountain and starry sky disappeared and was replaced by a square room with white walls similar to the corridor.

In front of Charlie was a door with the same markings as the one he had recently come through but, before he had a chance to try the same thing and press the winged pattern in the middle, the door opened straight up, sliding and disappearing into the ceiling.

There was a figure standing on the other side of where the door had been. As Charlie stared into the familiar eyes of the figure smiling at him, he collapsed to the floor, weakened, by the torrent of emotional confusion that overwhelmed him.

Jamie reached out a hand and helped Charlie to his feet.

∞

# Chapter VIII

## *The Reveal*

It took some time for Charlie to stop shaking and crying on his friend's shoulder. Eventually he managed to compose himself and Charlie stepped back wiping his face to look at his friend.

"I...I... just can't believe it!" stammered Charlie.

"Believe it" beamed Jamie. "Have I got some crazy shit to tell you!" he exclaimed.

"You were dead. I saw your eyes. They were lifeless," Charlie said.

"They're always lifeless," laughed Jamie. "But I wasn't dead, just sleeping that's all. Come on, let's get you cleaned up and then we'll get something to eat".

"Then you'd better tell what the hell is going on and where the hell we are?"

"We ain't in Kansas anymore Toto," joked Jamie. "Trust me mate, you are safe now and all will be revealed, come on."

∞

They exited the room and turned left down a corridor like the one Charlie had followed. From time to time, other people, men and women, walked passed them not giving them a second glance. They were dressed similarly; all white outfits like hospital surgeons. Some wore ties and white lab coats.

As they walked through a maze of winding corridors, they passed open doorways, which Charlie, could see led to other rooms where people were busy over computer screens and machinery unlike anything he had seen.

"Where are we?" he asked.

"Well, you won't believe this," said Jamie, "but we are actually in a spaceship".

Charlie's jaw dropped. "Bollocks", he said. "You're winding me up".

"I'm not!" laughed Jamie. "We are in a real-life spaceship; UFO, flying saucer, Death Star, the real article! Star Trek got it right, almost."

"But how?" stammered Charlie. "Is it top secret military or something? How is it possible?"

"Time travel," exclaimed Jamie. "I didn't believe it either until I saw it with my own eyes. Oh, here we are; our room."

The boys had stopped at another door but it was closed. The door was situated on the right of the corridor and on the left of the door was a small screen and above that, the letter 'E' and the number '4'. Jamie placed his hand flat on the screen and the door silently slid up into the ceiling.

"E4?" asked Charlie.

"Level E, Room 4" replied Jamie. "This ship is bloody big! Man-made as well, bloody amazing. None of your alien shit, although saying that, they do make good hover-skis."

"What are you talking about?" laughed Charlie.

Jamie smiled. "I've seen shit that'll make you piss yourself!" he said. "I promise I will tell you everything when you have had a shower because you stink. The medic will be here when you have finished to give you a quick check up then we will eat. What do you fancy, apart from Hannah Wilson?"

Charlie laughed. "Still the same Jamie. I could murder a fish and chips", realising how hungry he was.

"It will be done", Jamie said with an exaggerated bow. "Now go have your shower, it's over there."

∞

As Charlie stood under the warm spray and even with the water stinging his bruised knuckles, he felt his muscles relaxing and a wave of fatigue washed over him. His mind was racing with questions. A spaceship? Jamie alive? He quickly dried himself off, wrapped a towel around his waist and rejoined Jamie in what could only be described as the lounge.

"Put some clothes on" teased Jamie, shielding his eyes. "Here, these will do".

Jamie pointed to a pair of white overalls like the ones he was wearing and most of the people Charlie had seen. A pair of white Velcro fastening shoes finished the outfit.

After getting dressed in a room occupied by two double beds, Charlie was examined by a woman to see if he had sustained any breaks or internal damaging. He was also given an injection, which, he was told would slow down his ageing process. Jamie showed Charlie the same three-point puncture mark on his wrist, showing he had also had the injection.

After been given the all clear, Charlie joined Jamie at a dining table and, to Charlie's surprise, sat down to a perfect fish and chips complete with newspaper wrapping.

"Don't tell me you ordered in?" laughed Charlie.

Jamie smirked. "Nah, they have a machine that makes anything you want".

As they ate, Jamie told Charlie everything that had happened since they had fallen through the quarry floor.

∞

"Fortunately, I also landed in that river", said Jamie. "But when I washed up on that shore, four men were standing there. Before I could say anything, they put a needle to my neck and injected some sort of sedative probably, because I passed out."

"That's how I found you", interrupted Charlie, "but I passed out too".

"Well, it was while you were out that the men must have come back and carried me off, 'cause when I awoke, I was lying on the bed through there", Jamie pointed to the bedroom, "dressed in these white clothes. When I got up, a woman came into the room, said her name was Lisa and offered to be my guide. She was quite fit, so I couldn't refuse". Jamie smiled, had a drink from his Irn Bru can and carried on.

"We left the room and I followed Lisa down a series of corridors until we came to a huge room where lots of people were milling about. Around the walls were TV monitors with images of what looked like different periods of history. One would have a scene from Victorian times, another had dinosaurs on. I thought I was watching Jurassic Park! In the middle of the room was a huge circular table with loads of lines with dates on them. The table was lit with different colours and toy spaceships were moving back and forth along the datelines".

Charlie could not believe what he was hearing. As Jamie continued, a woman bought into the room two banana splits for the boys and took away their finished chip wrappers.

"Luxury", said Jamie. "Anyway, Lisa explained that we are on one ship of many actually hopping back and forth through time changing history and our future for the better".

Charlie took a scoop of ice cream but it hovered, poised near his mouth. Time travelling spaceships?

He gasped "This is unbelievable. How do you know that any of this is true?"

"I told you, I have seen it", whispered Jamie, "and I think it's time that you did too. Come on".

∞

# Chapter IX

## *The Reason*

Jamie got up and led Charlie out of their room into the corridor. As they walked, Jamie explained that they were in a Class Three Discovery Shuttle Cruiser from the 24th Century. Jamie smiled at Charlie's reaction.

Formerly NASA, the organisation unified with space exploration teams all over the globe in the beginning of the 22nd Century. The Earth was on the brink of an ecological disaster through a combination of global warming and man's continuous abuse of the planets resources.

The moon had already been colonised and further expeditions throughout the known solar system, began to recognise orbiting meteors and moons that could sustain human life.

Humankind spread out throughout the stars and science advanced.

Technology was at the forefront of man's mass exodus further into space, to escape the decaying earth.

As space exploration took Man further away from Earth, people realised they wanted to be closer to it. So, an Ecological Global Unity (EGU) was formed to decide how to reverse the planets demise.

It was agreed that prevention was better than a cure and so began the Time Quantum Experiment in the year 2275. Time travel had been successful in small amounts since 2230.

It was discovered that through the dilation of light particles in a contained nuclear field, the hydrogen atoms in light could be stretched, inflated, expanded to the extent where an object could move quicker than light and so, move forward in time.

This process was introduced to public transportation to reduce carbon emissions. However, as research was increased and advancement in time travel technology expanded, it was finally decided that EGU would use time-travel to travel back into the planet's past and directly study history for clues on how to prevent ecological damage. The theory was that it was possible to subliminally change the environment for the better.

A number of vital rules and laws were passed over five years until a constitution was drafted on how the experiment would be undertaken.

There would be ten small cruisers that would travel back in time and each reconnaissance a section of history. Once an environmental problem was recognised, an undercover team would influence the section of history for the better.

This was thought to be a flawless project as long as there was minimal effect on the past and without a negative knock-on effect for the future.

An initial voyage saw a small team travel back to 2012 to investigate the ozone layer, which in 2010 was at its thinnest. The team secretly infiltrated the world's governments and represented them at the 2012 Eco Summit in Tokyo, Japan.

As with the past two summits, Johannesburg in 2002 and Rio in 1992, representatives from participating countries would put forward ideas to assist the World in combating environmental concerns.

The EGU subtly put in place plans using 23rd Century technology to reverse the ozone layer depletion. Although the plans were thought to be extremely radical and too advanced, the worlds representatives (mostly EGU members), accepted it unanimously.

The project was nicknamed "Operation Ozone" and involved a two-part plan being undertaken. The first part saw an adaptation of weather satellites fitting them with modified solar panels that could bounce harmful rays from the sun away from the Earth.

The second part involved emitting natural chemical gases such as Carbon Dioxide into the atmosphere. The EGU introduced an emitter developed in the $22^{nd}$ century and passed it off as a $21^{st}$ century invention. The plan was to replace the dangerous gases that had built up.

It took just thirty years for the project to be completed. The EGU travelled back over the next millennium to keep an eye on the progress of the ozone layer. It was a huge success. The planet began to cool and icecaps began to reform. The planets ecosystems balanced out to a self-sustainable level, while skin cancer was non-existent. The knock-on effect for the future saw the colonisation of space move at a quicker rate as more time was spent on developing space travel rather than combating environmental problems.

Therefore, it seemed that if the EGU had not intervened in 2012, then they would not have had the opportunity to travel back in the first place.

∞

Charlie's mind whirled. "I don't get it at all!" he said. "How can they go back and do something that they couldn't do if they hadn't already done it? Bloody confusing!"

"It has something to do with parallel universes. Try not to figure it out," said Jamie. "I tried and I had a headache for two days. Just accept the fact that they know what they are doing and, it works."

"What do you mean, you had a headache for two days?" exclaimed Charlie. "How long has it been since we fell through the quarry?"

"It's only been three hours." Jamie laughed. "I've done a little bit of time travelling myself."

∞

# Chapter X

## *The Commander*

They arrived at the "map room" that Jamie had described earlier. A man approached, on them entering.

"Hello Jamie, everything ok?"

"Yeah, great Needles, thanks," replied Jamie shaking his hand. "This Needles, is Charlie."

Needles shook Charlie's hand. "Finally, I get to meet you. It is an extreme pleasure Sir. You are a legend in our time and I am honoured to have the opportunity to work with you."

"Erm, I don't mean to be rude," said Charlie "but what are you talking about?"

"Sorry," Needles replied. "I am a bit overwhelmed in meeting you. I'll explain.

∞

"I am Commander John Cunningham of the EGU's 21st Century reconnaissance team and you are aboard the *Blackbird*; a middle Class 3 Discovery Shuttle Cruiser."

"Told ya," interrupted Jamie.

Needles continued. "The *Blackbird* is one of ten ships time jumping between centuries attempting to rectify environmental problems for the benefit of mankind."

"Told ya that too!" Jamie whispered.

Commander Cunningham smiled. "I think it's best if you see for yourself."

Charlie followed Jamie and the commander down the short flight of stairs to the large circular map in the centre of the room.

"Do you see these lines?" The commander pointed to the various lines on the table. "They are the routes that our ships are taking through time. For example, this one here," and he indicated a green line dating from 2100-2150. "This is the *Phoenix*. It was the first of its kind, travelling back to 2010 and helping change the world for the better. It has been "hopping" for almost 30 years."

"Hopping?" asked Charlie.

"Hopping is what we call time travel" explained the commander "because we literally hop from one time to another. Sometimes it is just a brief visit, just for reconnaissance, other times we could be gone for years at a time but, thanks to almost instantaneous hopping, our families, friends, our own time do not miss us."

"But you must age?" said Charlie. "If you are away for long periods of time, when you got back, surely would be older than when you left?"

"Oh, we are, but ageing is now a choice not an inevitability in the 24th Century. It seems anti-wrinkle creams and the like were just the beginning of near-immortality. 50 years ago, in 2253, scientists finally discovered how to reduce ageing to an almost standstill. Hormones and steroids had to be used for centuries to speed up growth, particularly in babies born prematurely. So, all the scientists needed to do was figure out how to reverse the effects of steroids combined with the properties of anti-ageing products. It involved a chemical process of interlinking chemical compounds found naturally within the human body and with those of the anabolic and pro biotic steroids already on the market."

"Ageing is slowed down at a phenomenal rate since the discovery of a generic cure for all cancers in 2036, the eradication of the AIDS pandemic through artificial white blood cells in 2142, and the final global clearance of Avian Influenza H5N1/P3 in 2205. The human population has expanded at an incredible pace, hence the need for colonisation of other parts of space. The average lifespan is 175 years of both men and women."

"Amazing!" Charlie exclaimed.

"Yeah, tell me about it," said Jamie. "I still didn't believe it even after all that until Needles and his crew showed me what they're all about."

"Right, I think it is about time we showed you Charlie," said the commander. "Are you ready?"

"Yes, of course!" said Charlie excitedly. "I'm ready. It so difficult to believe all this. I feel like you're pulling my leg, all of you."

"Well relax," said the commander. You are perfectly safe and we are just about to pull your leg and the rest of you through time to...well, what do you want to see?"

"You mean we can go anywhere?" asked Charlie.

"We are in a time machine!" teased Jamie.

"Right...let's go back to *Jurassic Park*!" Charlie said with a smile.

∞

# Chapter XI

## *The Jump*

Jamie knowingly smiled back as the map room became a hive of activity. People began to press buttons and screens around the room began to change. Each of the monitors depicted either a huge area of forest, a wide grassy plain, or a vast wetland swamp area. From time to time movement could be seen on the screens as dinosaurs came into view. It was just like watching the film Jurassic Park.

"Stand by all stations" declared Commander Cunningham. "set co-ordinates for 75 million BC, location Vector 4 Alpha 2.9.

"What will be the middle of Texas, U.S.A.," exclaimed the commander turning to face Charlie. "We are not actually going to the Jurassic period", he continued. "The air during the Jurassic period is extremely toxic whereas the Cretaceous has a quality similar to ours. Do not worry, we have been there a number of times and it is perfectly safe."

Charlie nervously smiled and turned to face a large screen covering a wall opposite. It depicted a familiar landscape of rock.

"We are actually underneath the quarry that you fell through" said the commander.

"Commander Cunningham, how did you get there? Surely you can't pass though rock?"

"Please, call me Needles," said the commander. "No, we cannot pass through rock," he chuckled. "We send forward a scout prior to jump. They assess the Arrival Zones (AZ) suitable for the ship. We have a shield generator onboard that protects the ship from buffering during the jump.

"A Natural AZ is normally chosen as it does not tend to change too much over time. A natural underground water table formed the river you dropped into, more than 25,000 years ago. The river carved out the tunnel but also a huge cavern in which we are sitting in right now. We entered through a waterfall two miles east from here."

"That's *Deer Falls*," exclaimed Charlie.

"All systems are up and ready Commander," called out a woman at a desk in front of the large screen. "Co-ordinates are in place, cloaking shield on standby, and scouts are back reporting all clear for AZ."

The commander took a microphone from a stand. "Everyone be prepared to jump in thirty seconds. Engage engines."

Jamie took Charlie to a chair and as they sat down, Charlie began to hear the familiar rumbling again.

"It was the ship we heard up in the quarry," whispered Jamie. "They had just arrived when we were walking across the sand. They had come for us."

Charlie face was full of confusion when Jamie turned to him and winked. But before he could say anything, the rumbling got louder but fortunately not as loud as previous occasions. Charlie could feel the ship beginning to shake. The scene on the large screen began to move as the ship rotated round to the right. The picture on the screen changed to a view of the tunnel they were in. A familiar river stretched out in front of them leading to a dim light which they were approaching rapidly.

Jamie leaned over and whispered to Charlie. "The river that we fell in continued from where we were washed up and flowed under the ship." He was interrupted by the commander talking to the crew.

"Activate cloaking shield, extend drive fins, prepare to jump in 10."

Charlie looked at the screen. The light was getting closer and he could make out the inside of the waterfall.

"6!" stated one of the crew. They burst through the waterfall and the evening sun behind them cast shadows on the landscape but Charlie could not see the ships shadow.

"4!" The fields, trees, and roads below began to blur as if a watercolour painting had ran,

"3! Engaging TQE's"

"2!" the commander called.

"Hold onto your butt," Jamie smiled. "Here we go, you're gonna love this!"

"1! Mark!"

∞

# Chapter XII

## *The Rewind*

The rumbling immediately stopped. Charlie looked at the view beyond the ship. It was a blur of colour that was constantly changing.

"Recalibrate the image on screen" exclaimed the commander.

As Charlie watched, the picture cleared. He began to make out trees, water, mountains, all moving rapidly it seemed, underneath them. Also, as Charlie looked closer, the landscape was disappearing and reappearing. Mountain ranges were exploding up then a split second were not there. Vast expanses of water approached from the distance but by the time they were travelling over them, they were deserts or forests.

"What is going on?" whispered Charlie

"We're time travelling matey" Jamie replied excitedly. "We're travelling towards Texas physically, passing over the Atlantic but at the same time, travelling through erm...time! What we are seeing is the World changing rapidly over 75 million years, see?" Jamie pointed to the screen. A vast continent covered with snow and ice was splitting as the mountain range in the middle folded and parted like Moses and the Red Sea. The continent became two and drifted away from each other, turning a livid green as they did so.

"1 minute until AZ!" declared the woman sitting in front of the screen.

They were now passing over one of the land masses that had stopped drifting. Trees appeared and disappeared, rivers formed and dried.

"30 seconds!" said the woman.

They had stopped moving and were now watching the landscape go through its many guises as the years flew past.

"10 seconds!"

"All prepare for landing," said the commander.

"8! Reverse vertical engines"

"6! Bring the TQE's back into line." The rumbling began again and    Charlie saw the screen blur for a few seconds until an alien landscape came into focus.

"3!"

The first thing Charlie noticed was the mangrove swamp. A huge area stretching off into the distance full of tall trees with twisted branches and roots partly submerged in the dark water.

"2!"

It was not all swamp though. Charlie saw to the left a rich green grassed plain split by a river, leading off to vast wooded forest some three miles away.

"1! Mark!" With the slightest shudder, the view stopped moving, the rumbling stopped, and all was still.

"Retain cloaking shield," the commander announced. "Patrick, Wilson, report to Expedition Bay 2 and get kitted up for re-con."

Two men's faces appeared on a small screen next to the commander.

"Yes Sir," they both said.

Commander Cunningham turned his chair to face Charlie. "Are you ready to believe?" he asked.

"Absolutely," said Charlie.

The commander led the two boys out of the map room and along the corridor.

"Every safety precaution is in place so you've nothing to worry about" he said. "We have on board a squad of 100 TQE Support troops, trained to combat any situation. Of course, the most dangerous time period is the one we have come to. Humans are easier to control than dinosaurs." He laughed, but Charlie just felt more nervous. "Relax," the commander said in reaction to Charlie's face. "Our boys will look after you."

They entered an elevator that took them down to level V and the Expedition Bays. The lift door opened and the three stepped out into a vast warehouse. Charlie felt like he was standing in a cross between an aircraft hangar, a store room, and a car garage. Boxes and containers were stacked on the floor while multiple shelves aligned the walls. A variety of vehicles and technical equipment was also scattered about the bay.

On the far side a huge door was open but a familiar wall of light obscured his view to the outside.

"An electro-magnetic force field," the commander explained.

"Virtually impassable unless hit by and object moving at a large velocity."

"I ran through one of them," Charlie said.

"We were monitoring your every move from the cave," said the commander. "We broke the circuit just enough for an instant otherwise you would have broken your shoulder. A look of realisation spread over Charlie's face. "If you were monitoring my every move, then why didn't you help me?" He was becoming angry.

"Because," The commander said with an innocent look on his face.

"We were testing you!" he exclaimed.

"Testing me? Why?" but before Charlie could get his answer, he was approached by two men wearing outfits like 21st Century British Army.

"Gentlemen, these are Sergeants Joe Patrick and Steve Wilson" the commander said introducing the men in front of them.

"We have completed a check of the surrounding area Sir." Wilson declared. "It is clear of any immediate threat. There are a number of large sauropods on the South bank of the river, with a mixed herd of smaller herbivores including *Triceratops* and *Stegosaurs*. There are also a few *Compy's* around but nothing to be concerned about."

"Negative signs of *Raptors* or other carnivores," added Patrick and oxygen, toxin, and acid levels are at an acceptable balance."

"Good," exclaimed the commander. "Get Charlie and Jamie kitted out and escort them outside for a look. Keep the trip to 30 minutes. If anything seems not right or out of place, return immediately to the ship."

"Yes Sir."

"Squad 3 and 4 will go with you. Standard A Class formation once outside. You will be in radio and visual contact so report back as routine, every 5 minutes, ok?"

"Yes Sir, will do."

"Good." The commander once again turned to Charlie. You are going to love this," he smiled. "Look after him Jamie."

"Will do Needles," saluted Jamie. "He's gonna be fine."

The commander smiled, turned on his heal and left in the elevator.

∞

Fifteen minutes later the boys were dressed in camouflage overalls, black walking boots and were adorned with a selection of equipment; a radio, respirator and a compact O2 tank, first aid kit, torch and an electrically charged extendable rod for self-defense.

Another eight similarly dressed people joined them.

"This is Squad 3 and 4," exclaimed Sergeant Patrick. "They will be escorting and protecting us while we are out of the ship." Each person was carrying a large rifle.

"Deactivating cloaking shield," a voice announced over a tannoy. The squads lined up and formed a circle around the two boys, Patrick and Wilson.

"Here we go!" said Jamie excitedly.

The squad member at the front approached a panel to the left of the wall of light. She took her glove off and placed her hand on it. The wall disintegrated and Charlie followed the team out into the sunlight.

∞

# Chapter XIV

## *The Past*

A wall of heat hit the boys as they followed the squads down an embankment on to the grassy plain below. The air was humid and alive with flying insects. Most of them were smaller than your fingernail but one or two were as large as a sparrow. As Charlie stood aghast, an impressive looking dragonfly with an 8-inch wingspan flew past his goggles, causing him to fall back onto the bank. One of the squad members helped him up and as the ground levelled out, Charlie looked back at the ship they had just left.

Every spacecraft, rocket, space shuttle, UFO, or spy plane that he had ever seen on TV or in magazines made up the *Blackbird*. It was huge! A white wall loomed up in front of Charlie, stretching 100ft up. The ship stretched to the left and right to almost a mile. It was shaped like, what Charlie thought, was a large door wedge. At one end to the right, the ship was a vast skyscraper reaching to the heavens. It stretched along and down to the other end, tapering to a point. The ship was resting on several hydraulic metal skids and it was adorned with a huge cylindrical observation tower on the top. Toward the front, covering the tower, can only be described as radio masts and what Charlie could not see was at the back of the ship, there were six huge round exhaust ports, now making pinging sounds as they cooled. On the side of the observation tower painted black, was the letters "C3" followed by the word in italics, *Blackbird.*

"Told you it was big," said Jamie.

"Gentleman, shall we?" asked Patrick. The boys turned back to the field and continued to follow the team towards the river.

As they walked, Charlie began to make out movement on the other side of the river. His binoculars had taken a battering during his journey but they still worked and as Charlie bought them up to his eyes, he gasped with amazement.

Drinking at the edge of the river on the far bank was a huge dinosaur, its long neck tipping up to swallow water. It was as large as two double decker buses and was a green, brown colour all over. As it drank, it was joined by another nine dinosaurs of the same species but of different sizes.

The first one looked up as the team approached the opposite bank. It let out a deep bellow and continued to drink.

Charlie stood with his mouth open in amazement. As he watched, smaller dinosaurs came down to the water all along the bank. Charlie recognised a small herd of *Stegosaurs* with their line of vertical plates running over their backs. A trio of *Triceratops* were grazing on the edge of the wood behind; their huge horns were swaying from side to side as they fed.

An Apatosaurus with its single curved vocal horn came into view and as if to confirm Charlie's theory, it let out a loud trumpet like call, which resonated across the valley. A young calf joined it and both went to the water to drink.

"This is unbelievable!" exclaimed Charlie. "They are real dinosaurs!"

*Lewis Davies*

"Incredible, isn't it?" laughed Jamie. "Now do you believe?"

Charlie nodded not being able to say anything. He watched the animals moving, grazing, and drinking. 75 Million Years into the past, Charlie now stood looking at some of the largest animals to have walked the planet and, as he turned and smiled at Jamie, Charlie's mind cleared and realisation dawned on him. All the uncertainty of what he wanted to do in life, careers advise at school, studies, was wiped from his mind.

"I want to talk to the commander."

"I thought you might," smiled Jamie.

∞

# Chapter XV

## *The Future*

Back on the ship, Charlie and Jamie had got changed and were now sitting at a long rectangular table in a large room decorated with framed photos from history. Also at the table were three men including Commander Cunningham.

"This is Captain Jeffreys," the commander said, pointing to the man on his left, "and on my right, is Flight Lieutenant Miske."

"We have been travelling through time" said Jeffreys "We do not alter history; that is the job of Sector 6; Georgeson and her crews. What we do is study the history books and anything else that may have information on the Earth's past, so a lot of our work is administration."

However, if you excuse the pun, a huge proportion of our "time" is spent in different eras, undercover. We investigate and record first hand issues that are under scrutiny. We then assess what course of action should be undertaken and contact Control who sends out a crew from Section 6 or *The Architects*, as we like to call them. Sometimes we are away for years!"

"Control?" asked Charlie. "Are they the ones in charge?"

"Control is the brain centre of the whole operation," said Lieutenant Miske. "The EGU's main headquarters are back in the 24<sup>th</sup> Century. We have bases located throughout time. There are fuel stations, medical labs, briefing rooms, ship and equipment repair, even living accommodation for up to 5000 crew. All secret, all safe."

"Commander," a voice came over the tannoy. "Co-ordinates are set for the homeward jump on your command. Plus, a herd of *Brontosaurs* are beginning to take an interest in the ship!"

"Understood," the commander, replied. "Engage TQE's in 30. Would all crew prepare for Jump? Thank you."

The commander looked at Jamie and Charlie. "I know this must be overwhelming for you both but it is imperative that you know "everything".

It is not pure chance that bought you to the ship. We came to find you." The commander continued. "Jamie, I know you know that but the true reason shall be revealed when we get back to Control. It is not for me to tell you. You will need to meet the heads of the operation. That is if you have no objections returning with us to the year 2303?"

Jamie and Charlie looked at each other and smiled.

"I will take that as a yes then?" the commander asked, smiling back as the boys nodded eagerly.

∞

"3, 2, 1, Mark!" came the voice again over the tannoy. From outside, the dinosaurs taking an interest in the ship, bolted with terror as the ship rose vertically up on its huge thrusters located underneath the ship. As it gained height, the six rear engines swung down to provide extra power and in a second, the ship was out of sight of the dinosaurs as it broke through the atmosphere and out into deep space.

Charlie did not have time to gasp in amazement because the ship suddenly halted and then began to move forward. The view out of the large screen in the map room was one of bright lines passing by all around them. A digital counter was underneath the screen and the numbers were rolling round at a blurred rate. If Charlie had been in the map room, he would not have believed what he saw now displayed on the many monitors around the room.

Each one depicted the 24th Century. Towering buildings of white came into view, glass domes, and vehicles zipping around the global metropolis that was Earth. The moon blinked with a billion lights. It seemed as if the stars in the sky were moving with irregularity as ships Jumped from one part of the galaxy to another using hyper-propulsion. Apart from small, restricted Time Quantum Engines in public transport, time travel was now restricted to the EGU and standard space travel was through Hydro-methane based fuel emitting a power stronger than nuclear. With the combination of solar power and a water-based coolant, ships engines powered by Hydro-methane were environmentally sound and able to transport a ship through space in almost an instant.

Around the Earth, thousands of satellites had turned their panels toward the sun and the planet's atmosphere constantly blinked where ships came and went.

As Charlie and Jamie re-entered the map room, they saw on the large screen a vast space station appeared as the *Blackbird* slowed back down. Around the space station, ships similar to the *Blackbird* were docked at various appendages protruding from the huge circular structure slowly spinning on its axis. Vehicles were constantly arriving and departing at smaller docking stations and not unlike insects, robotic remotes crawled over the exterior of the space station, sending off brief sparks as they carried out repair work.

"This is Control," announced Commander Cunningham proudly. It is the main base of the EGU. The size of the United Kingdom, Control is a civilisation in itself and is the epicentre of all space exploration and humankind's expansion into the stars.

"The TQE Experiment was developed here and Controls ancestor was the original Meer Space Station built by the Russians back in the 20th Century.

Over the centuries, more has been added and at the creation of EGU, Control was born."


"AZ 3 is open and awaiting our arrival, Commander," came the voice over the tannoy.

"Very good," the commander replied into his own intercom. "Bring her in to dock and contact Admiral Aziz. Ask him to meet us in Briefing room 12. It is time you two knew the whole truth and why we came to find you," he said, turning to Charlie and Jamie.

Charlie and Jamie were led back to their room and after having time to go to the bathroom, were met by Commander Cunningham and Captain Jeffreys.

"Ready gentleman?" the commander asked smiling.

"Lead on," Charlie said. "I am ready for anything!"

They were escorted back down to the expedition bays but the one they arrived at was not like a warehouse as before but a carpeted wide corridor. At the end of the corridor was an open door and the corridor continued beyond.

As they walked down it, the commander explained the origins of the space station. He was interrupted however, when the corridor came to an end and opened into a futuristic world of turbo lifts, walkways, sliding doors, and thousands of people going about their business. They were talking, walking, entering and exiting lifts, carrying piles of paper, small cases, boxes, bags, and all were wearing the same uniforms as Charlie and Jamie.

"Welcome to Control and the 24th Century," stated the commander.

Charlie and Jamie stood open mouthed. Leaning on a handrail, they looked across their new world and both smiled.

∞

# Chapter XVI

## *The Control*

From their position at the handrail, Charlie and Jamie could see across a vast city. They were on one of a thousand levels that wove their way across the cavernous metropolis. Above them, the walkways disappeared beyond sight, below, the city stretched to unseen depths. Everywhere the boys looked, there was movement. Turbo lifts transported people vertically and horizontally across the city and Charlie saw various objects moving around that were unmistakably robots.

They were different shapes and sizes, all with what seemed different purposes. Some were carrying things; others were pushing or towing metal pallets of boxes. There were small robots that buzzed around in the air like insects and there were huge human shaped robots that lumbered around, towering over the people that were making their way along in the robot's shadow.

As Charlie and Jamie watched, a floating platform the shape and size of a train carriage came toward them from their right and flew to a standstill in front of them, its door disappearing into its roof in a way the boys had now become accustomed to.

"Our transport has arrived," announced Commander Cunningham.

With that, a small bridge extended and slipped its way under the walkway they were standing on. A section of the handrail slid into itself and Commander Cunningham led the boys onto the platform.

They found themselves some seats fixed to the platform and sat down.

The handrail slid back into place, the bridge retracted and the platform moved off smoothly away from the walkway, its door silently closing.

As they gently glided through the air, Charlie gazed through the window as if in a dream. He hardly heard Commander Cunningham's voice as the commander explained the architecture of the station.

"Control is really just a small part of the station but it still covers an area the size of Wales. The rest of the station is dedicated to the living facilities of 2 million people. It is the centre of our ship construction and the base for all the repairs. Our research labs are located here several levels up, and storage facilities stretch over a quarter of the whole station. There are 6000 holosuites where we carry out training and research and the station even has its own mountain range, rivers and two rainforests."

Charlie followed Jamie and the Commander in a daze and only remembered he was not alone when Jamie shouted, "Mind the door!"

Charlie snapped out of his trance just as the turbo lift doors closed in front of him.

"We are heading up to the offices of our Heads of State," said Commander Cunningham. "They are the founders of EGU and have been overseeing and coordinating its progress for 30 years. The World owes everything to their vision, ambition, and their passion to save the planet."

After ten minutes, the door of the turbo lift eventually opened and the occupiers were greeted by a woman in a red suit like the white ones everyone else had been wearing.

"Welcome gentleman," she said. "We have been expecting you. My name is Amanda Stanton, I am the P.A. to Messrs. Davies and Young."

"What?!" exclaimed Charlie and Jamie at the same time, just as a pair of large doors opened in front of them and the boys looked on two men with two extremely familiar faces.

∞

# Chapter XVII

## *The Mirror*

Charlie and Jamie stood motionless in the doorway, not able to believe what they were seeing. Standing in front of them were themselves but looking 40 years older. Jamie's older version was broader in the shoulders than the 17-year-old. The man had cropped grey hair and a short full grey beard. He wore a black patch over his left eye.

Charlie gazed down at his older self because the man was sitting in a wheelchair. From the knee down, he was missing his right leg and in place of it was a metal limb. He had the same colour hair as Charlie, short and spiked. His face looked tired but there was a spark behind the eyes. He was clean-shaven apart from a thin goatee and a large deep scar the length of his right cheek.

"Welcome," he said, "to your future".

"You are me and he is you!" Charlie gasped pointing to his older self and the two Jamie's. "What is going on? How are you here and we are here?"

It was Jamie's older self that spoke first.

"We have been involved with the EGU since its beginnings 30 years ago but time travel has helped us make a positive difference for centuries. We are 90 years your senior but we are 300 years into your future."

They all sat down at a round table in the middle of the room. Commander Cunningham joined them along with another man introduced as Admiral Aziz. Amanda Stanton bought in refreshments as the older Jamie continued.

"This will all become apparent to you in time but for now, it is vital that you listen very closely to what we have to say. It may be very confusing for you to sit here now and be talking to us and believe me; we know exactly how you feel. I remember thinking I looked really old!"

The younger Jamie smiled. "I do think you look old."

"I remember saying that too," replied the older Jamie. "We have been waiting for this meeting for 90 years and it has been an interesting 90 years!"

As if in response to the confusion in their faces, the elder Jamie reminded them of the age reducing technology that they were subjected to earlier. "The injections you received earlier have done us well. They slowed down our ageing process, which has allowed us to achieve so many of the plans that fate had laid down in front of us.

"We were present in Tokyo when the decision was passed to undertake Operation Ozone. We witnessed the scrapping of the last petrol and diesel vehicles in the year 2026. We were on board the *Phoenix* when it took its first jump back to the last ice age, 11000 years ago. There, we placed on each continent several 1000 huge thermal regulators that proceeded to reverse the effects of the ice age and bring the planet's surface temperature back to a temperate level. Without this intervention, mankind would not have survived the last ice age and humanity would have become extinct."

Jamie put his hand up at this point. "If the last ice age would have wiped out the human race, how could you go back to prevent it happening in the first place?"

"Time is not set," replied his older self. "There are many timelines that create the history of the Universe and many more can be made through subtle changes in their past. When we travelled back to the last ice age, we followed a timeline that ran parallel with the one that would have been created if we had not intervened. If we had not succeeded in our mission, the original timeline would have been the only route back and we would have returned to a future with no human life.

"It is a paradoxical concept that can test even our most respected Time Physicians. Professor Davies and I have spent several years studying time and its rudiments, developing the art of time travel, advising on what action would be needed when jumping to different parts of history and even conceptually designing the ship that brought you here. We have been part of the research team spending many long hours sifting through history books, viewing footage of Earth's history from political to environmental. Professor Davies alone came up with the concept of the Time Quantum Experiment and, although he obviously heard about it here as you," he pointed to Charlie,

"Professor Davies elaborated on the idea of time travel and began to turn the theory into reality, but I am sure he can explain the finer details to you himself."

*Lewis Davies*

It was at this point, that Charlie realised that his older self, had not said a word since they met. He sat in his wheel chair leaning on his elbows at the end of the table with his fingers bridged in front of his mouth. Charlie saw that he had a wedding ring on.

As Charlie looked over the man, his eyes scanned over his face and suddenly realised that the Professor was staring right at him. Charlie quickly averted his gaze back to Professor Young who continued to speak.

"There is a crack in one of the timelines," he said. "This has been caused by a globally influential event occurring long before it is supposed to.      For example, the last ice age occurred 11,000 years ago. After extensive studies of its timeline and reoccurring visits to that period, we calculated that it should not have occurred for another 6 million years. Hence why we had to intervene. Man's evolution would have continued but the crack in the timeline threatened that evolution. This latest crack seems to have the same potential to have a devastating effect on all life on Planet Earth. The thing is, we cannot foresee what this crack is. We have an idea because cracks cause time echoes. We have found some small evidence of the rift in the timeline here, in our time. All the evidence points to a global disaster that, unless is repaired, will continue to send out time echoes that will grow larger and larger until the evidence left behind will engulf our time and become the future that is at the end of the fractured timeline. We have tried to analyse the crack by travelling back to a point in time after the crack has occurred but any of our ships that take the trip, have never came back. They are still out there somewhere, lost in time."

"The only jumping now we are able to do is to travel back to the point of the cracks origin. After that, we have found it impossible to jump to any period after the crack occurs. We lost a lot of ships and brave men and women," The commander said sadly.

They sat there in silence for a while until Jamie decided to ask, "this global disaster, when do you think it may happen, in the past I mean?"

"We are not for certain," replied Professor Young, "but we have made some calculations and we have discovered that the crack in the timeline occurred in 2010."

"2010?" Charlie exclaimed. "That is the year that Jamie and I have just left, just before we arrived here!"

"That is why you are here!" The statement came from the top of table and Charlie turned to look at his older self.

∞

# Chapter XVIII

## *The Plan*

Professor Davies' voice, although quiet and soft, resonated across the room. A gruffness to it made Charlie feel sorry for him. It seemed as if he was tired and every syllable uttered took great effort to pronounce.

For the first time Charlie gave his older self a smile and to his relief, the smile was returned and although somewhat with less enthusiasm, there was an equal respect.

"We have been waiting to meet you for 90 years," Professor Davies reiterated. The crack in the time line is so severe there was only one moment in your life that we could hone in on you. The crack appeared soon after you fell at the quarry. Anywhere on your timeline, after that moment is unstable and impossible to locate. Plus, Professor Young and I remember the first encounter with your destiny as if it was only yesterday and for you, it was!"

As if to answer their question, Professor Davies continued.

"It is your destiny to be here, it was your destiny to fall in that quarry, even to leave your houses that fateful morning."

"Commander Cunningham said earlier that you were testing me," Charlie said.

"We had to be sure that we had located the right you," the Professor continued. The crack in the time line was creating multiple futures for yourselves. I remember falling into the river. I remember feeling my way through the dark tunnels of the ships storage area, I remember finding Jamie's lighter and making my way out through one of the holo-decks. There could only be one version of my younger self to achieve that. Any other version of the events leading up to now would not be the true history as I remember it so the following decisions you make from now on would not have been the right ones and would have disastrous repercussions. Understand?"

"Kind of," replied Charlie.

"You are the true versions of our past and it is you that will repair the crack in the timeline. In our history, it has already happened but should you fail, our history will be rewritten, the crack will become larger and engulf our shared timeline. Even though this is your future, it can be altered by the decisions you make from now on."

"What is this new crack? Jamie asked.

"We cannot say exactly," replied Professor Young. "But we are discovering more and more evidence in our own time to suggest it may be another ice age of global proportions. Back in the 21st century Climate change caused by man's careless actions was the beginning of one of these ice ages.      Although it seemed as if the planet was warming up, the melting of the polar caps would have caused a global increase in surface water cooling the planet down, particularly when landmasses were submerged. The EGU hypothesised this may happen so put measures in place before the situation became irreversible. This was called "Operation Ozone". As the impending ice age was not a result of a crack in the timeline, we were able to jump through Earth's history and future that flanked the particular moment in time when the ice age would occur."

"An ice age!" Jamie exclaimed. "How are we going to stop an ice age? We are just two lads!"

"We will help you as far as we can," said Professor Davies. "However, inevitably, it will be you two alone that will carry out the task. It is already written in our history." He indicated to himself and Professor Young.

"What task?" Charlie asked. He was beginning to feel a bit light-headed and overwhelmed.

"We need you to plant an explosive device at a core site," Said Professor Young. "The device is the key to your success and the future of all life on Earth."

"No pressure then," scoffed Jamie.

"What is this device?" asked Charlie.

"This crack in the timeline is not only affecting your future," said Commander Cunningham, "but also our future! 340 years from now, EGU scientists will develop a bomb that, on explosion, will emit a mushroom cloud of liquid Nitrogen and Frontium. This compound was developed as part of the cryogenic programme of 2204 to provide cryo-status units for space travel. Before the initial development of time travel some 30 years later, man had been travelling across the stars in real time. This would understandably cause extreme ageing as some trips were up to 10 years each way. If you remember what was said earlier, we did not discover the secret of anti-ageing until the end of the last century so Cryogenics was adapted for space travel.

Placing an individual into suspended animation, essentially shutting down all life signs except the heart and brain, was a successful way, if a little risky, of slowing down the ageing process.

*Lewis Davies*

"The chemical elements involved with Cryogenics, Nitrogen and Frontium, were treated separately. Liquid Nitrogen was produced by fractional distillation of liquid air while Frontium atoms were individually mutated in a nuclear reactor by firing photons in to their nuclei causing the molecules to expand. Then it was a simple chemical process of combining Liquid Nitrogen molecules with the expanded Frontium particles to create a new compound. The new compound had the qualities of liquid nitrogen in that if kept just above -210°C, the liquid would not solidify and would have cryogenic characteristics, namely causing instant freezing on contact but it also had the expanded Frontium molecules amplifying the effects of the Liquid Nitrogen.

The fluid was sealed in a vacuumed container, which was then inserted into an 8-inch canister along with a nuclear charge. The charge was in place to make sure that the liquid compound spread over a vast area. It would be carried through the air by the blast and by the subsequent mushroom cloud that followed. Although the fallout would not be substantial enough to cover the 5 million square miles of the target area, the cloud would blanket a large enough area with frozen particles to halt the advance of the ice age."

Charlie and Jamie looked at each other.

"This is a lot to take in," Charlie said. "If I understand this right, you want us to place a nuclear bomb filled with freezing liquid at a strategic site somewhere around the World so its explodes and covers the place in frozen particles thus stopping an ice age?!"

"That is correct," replied his older self.

"Where exactly is this site?" Charlie asked.

The face of Professor Davies seemed to go dark and there was a general uneasiness between the two facing Charlie and Jamie.

Professor Davies sighed and bowed his head as if recalling some distant memory that he would prefer to forget. He eventually raised his head and with sadness in his eyes, he said.

"Antarctica!"

# Chapter XIX

## *The Professor*

They all left Briefing Room 12 and, apart from Ms. Stanton walking behind, Charlie and Jamie finally got to be alone with their older selves as Commander Cunningham and Admiral Aziz said their goodbyes and left.

"I have an appointment with Anatomy Reconstruction, would you mind accompanying me?" asked Professor Davies to Charlie.

"Not at all," said Charlie. "Do you mind Jamie?"

"No worries," Jamie replied. "I have a lot to ask myself, I'll see you shortly".

He and Professor Young entered a turbo-lift and left Charlie and his older self alone.

They exited the corridor they were in, through an arched doorway out onto one of the many walkways.

"I know you have many questions Charlie," his older self said. "I know what you are thinking and I know what I will say to you. It is a strange feeling even now, seeing you. I remember being where you are now and hearing what I am saying to you and I thought that I would be prepared for this meeting but I was not. So many years have passed by for me, thinking of what I would say, trying to remember word for word how I heard it all those years ago, writing countless notes and sentences but now that moment is upon me again with roles reversed, I am hearing it exactly as I remember it."

Charlie saw his older self smile, if only for an instant.

"It seems as if I had nothing to worry about. I even remember me saying that, and that, Christ, I could go on!" He allowed himself a light chuckle but then, the moment of carefree passed and his face returned to the sad, remorseful look that was beginning to make Charlie feel uneasy.

They approached a railing, which swung out on to the small bridge of a transport platform identical to the one they had travelled on earlier. The Professor locked the wheels of his chair in place as Charlie sat down and the platform moved off.

"Where are we going?" Charlie asked.

"The Medical levels," replied the Professor. "I am in the final stages of my leg reconstruction and today needs to be it. That is correct, isn't it Ms. Stanton?"

Charlie had not noticed but the professors P.A. had been with them the whole time and was currently sitting behind them on the platform.

"Yes Sir," she replied. "I have spoken to Doctor Grant and he has assured me that your leg will be completely reconstructed and fully functioning by the launch tomorrow."

"Excellent," said Professor Davies. He turned to Charlie. "My leg," he said, "has had 3 operations so far. One to have it amputated, one to have this put in place," he tapped the metallic limb that was in place of his lower right leg, and the third operation was to reconstruct and reanimated the nerves, veins, and tendons that have been severed just below the knee cap. They have been attached to my new lower leg and God willing, I will be as right as rain for the launch."

"Ok," said Charlie. "I have two questions to start with. The first one is what launch are you talking about? Second one is, and please stop me if it is too personal but, how did you lose your leg?"

At the mention of the second question, the Professors face again went remorseful, as if he had lost more than his leg.

"I will answer your first one now but I think if we are going to discuss my past, i.e. your future then; a) I need a new leg first and b) I need a drink!
Time is running out, for all of us and action needs to be taken now. The time echoes are getting larger each day. We must leave tomorrow and head back to 2010. In five days, if you and Jamie have not succeeded then there will literally be no time to save!"

The Professor paused for a moment, then continued. "The launch we have been talking about is ours on the *Blackbird*. Commander Cunningham has volunteered to assist us and Jump Time is 2:00pm tomorrow afternoon. Both Professor Young and I are with you, plus Sergeant Patrick and his team of Tactical Support will be coming along as well.

"We also have an external team travelling from the 28th century and will be waiting for us on Earth somewhere."

"What do you mean somewhere?" Charlie said suspiciously.

"We received a very faint signal sent from their homing beacon but the exact location is inaccurate as the tectonic plates have shifted since the signal was transmitted thus shifting the origins location."

"Well, can't you ask them to send the message again?" Charlie asked.

"We would if we could," replied the Professor, "but radio waves will only travel forwards through time and their trajectory cannot be reversed."

"Ok," said Charlie. "How long is the radio signal? I mean, how long has it been transmitting? If they are waiting for us then that means..."

The professor interjected. "That's right. They have been waiting 297 years!"

∞

# Chapter XX

## *The Accident*

Charlie thought about this for a few minutes as they floated along through the shining city.

Finally, he said, "Why didn't the ship just come back to this time from 2010 and discuss in person where to meet?"

"The time echoes have become so severe, it would have been impossible for them to locate this stage in the timeline. The crack has prevented any time travel forward from 2010 to be too dangerous and would have serious implications for the existing timelines."

"So, if they cannot travel back to their own time or to here, then they are stuck in 2010!" exclaimed Charlie.

"Yes", replied the professor. "They are all risking never to see their own family or friends again to save their own future and in doing so, have taken a one-way trip to a yet, undecided past."

"So where do you think they are?" asked Charlie.

"We know where they are." The older man said. "Remember, for Professor Young and I, it has already happened. We have co-ordinates of the precise location of the ship but the crack in the timeline will affect our navigation equipment so jumping to the precise co-ordinates will not be possible. We have a 10-mile radius of accuracy which, is the best we can do."

"So, where are they?" Charlie asked.

His older self turned to him. "The South American jungle!"

∞

Charlie's mind was still racing when they arrived at one of the thousands of medical centres that stretched across the stations 476th level.

As they left the transport platform and headed for the open door of the centre, Charlie finally plucked up the courage to ask his older self the question that he wanted to ask when he first saw him.

"Professor," he said. "I hope you don't mind me asking but, how did you lose your leg?"

The professor seemed to hesitate for a moment as if he was disinclined to answer but then as they entered the large white building, he spoke.

*Lewis Davies*

"Professor Young and I were accompanying a reconnaissance team back to the Cretaceous period with the intention of collecting some samples.    We had found that some species of wetland plant from that era could trap oxygen and store it. We were studying their qualities in an effort to create artificial gills to assist our Marine Division.

"It was meant to be a routine trip but we...ran into some difficulty."

The professor seemed to falter as if it pained him to continue but he did.

"We were exploring the woodland that bordered a marshy area. The team had split into two sections, Professor Young with one a few yards away and I was with the other. All the pre-checks had been carried out, and the teams we were with had several jumps of experience between them."

Charlie and the professor followed Ms. Stanton who had been joined by a nurse, down the corridors of the hospital. Professor Davies was now being assisted as a hospital orderly walked behind the professor's chair pushing it along. As they went further and further into the hospital via corridors, turbo lifts and conveyors, Professor Davies continued.

"We were attacked," he said. "We did not see it coming. They must have stalked us through the forest because they came at us from behind and knew exactly what they were doing."

"What did?" asked Charlie

"Velociraptors!" the Professor replied. "Pack hunters. They were 5 feet tall bipeds with the speed of a cheetah and the deadliness of a great white shark. The velociraptor was one of the most ferocious dinosaurs to have ever existed."

He paused for a moment. It was clear to Charlie that the professor was finding it difficult talking about it.

Professor Davies continued. "There were five of them and they all attacked at the same time. I was knocked to the ground by one and as I tried to get up, it grabbed my leg and began to drag me away from my team. If it wasn't for Lance Corporal Evans I would have been dead. He fired his pulsar rifle at the animal four times before it eventually let go, taking my leg with it and fled back into the forest. Two of the other raptors were killed while the rest retreated after the one that attacked me. I lost more than my leg that day; seven of our team were killed including my son, Jason."

Charlie felt himself begin to well up and he placed a comforting hand on the Professor's shoulder.

They carried on down the corridor in silence for some time until they finally arrived at the Anatomy Reconstruction department.

"Good day professor," said a Doctor going by the name of Dr. Saunders. "How is the new leg baring up?"

"It is ok thanks, Doc" Said Professor Davies. I will be happier when it is covered."

"Today," said Dr. Saunders with a friendly smile. "Today is the day. The wound seems to have healed fine and your upper leg has accepted the artificial limb well. So, now it is time to get it covered."

Charlie followed the professor into a cubicle where a male nurse helped the professor change into a surgical gown and attached a cannula to his left hand.

"During the operation, I am afraid you will have to wait outside the theatre," said the nurse. "I hope you understand?"

"Of course," Charlie said. "Good luck Professor."

Another nurse came and wheeled the professor off to theatre and as Ms. Stanton went to get a coffee, Charlie was left alone for the first time since being on the holodeck, and he felt terrified.

His mind was filled to exploding and he reeled with the effort of coming to terms with where he was, what he was being asked to do, and the fact that he had had a son that had been killed!

Charlie felt his eyes water but he quickly wiped the tears away as Ms. Stanton came back with two cups of coffee. She handed one to him and placed a hand on his shoulder.

"I know this is overwhelming for you," she said. "But, you are a strong person. I have known you for 15 years and you are the bravest, most determined man I have ever met. Just remember that you do succeed in your mission, otherwise this time would not exist."

"So why do I have to do this?" cried Charlie. "Why do I have to watch my son die? I'm only 17 and I have been told that I have a son who dies in front of me and I save the planet from an environmental disaster and if I don't, then everyone's future is destroyed! I don't think I can do this." Charlie put his head in his hands to hide his tears.

"You have to succeed!" Ms. Stanton said. "You will succeed. It is written but time is running out and both history and the future are being re-written the more you doubt yourself."

They both sat in silence for a moment. Charlie lifted his head from his hands and took a drink of coffee from his cup.

It was hard for Charlie to imagine that he was saviour of the human race. He was just a boy. He had not even passed his driving test. And now he had been plunged into a world he did not know and was expected to carry out the ultimate task.

They say that "it is written", that "it has already happened". How do they know that he will do it this time? The crack in the timeline grows bigger every day but it is all happening so far into my future, why should I care? Then Charlie's thoughts turned to his older self. He was to become that man. The man that everyone respected, believed in, almost religiously had faith in. He would become one of the founders of the EGU and a pioneer of time travel. He was everything that Charlie would wish to be and strived to be, so why was he so apprehensive about fulfilling his destiny?

Then it dawned on him. He did not want to see his son die. He had an overwhelming love for someone who he had not yet met and like all fathers, felt he would do anything for his son. He could not bear the thought of losing someone he already felt so close to and suddenly, Charlie had an idea.

What if he could save his son? Yes, it was many years into his future but he could wait and he could change the course of his future. He knew what was going to happen and he could intervene. Stop his son going on the mission. Then reality dawned on him. It had already happened for his older self. His son had died in the raptor attack and he had lost his leg. The evidence was in the next room! But the crack in the timeline caused everything to be undecided. It was causing the future to change, to mutate, so why couldn't Charlie do the same? The EGU had been subtly influencing the past for the better over the centuries and it dawned on Charlie that he could influence his own future for the better.

Charlie felt a surge of adrenalin suddenly course through him. A new determination and confidence overwhelmed him and he seemed to finally accept that this was his destiny, his fate and in that moment, his decision was made.

∞

# Chapter XX1

## *The Album*

The door of the theatre room opened and a nurse came out. "Professor Davies is anaesthetised," she said, "and we are about to begin the reconstruction surgery to his leg. It is a simple process of sculpting a silicon-based model of his lower leg and wrapping it around the artificial endoskeleton he has already in place. We take a 3D polygraphic x-ray of his other leg and create a mirror image, replicating each curve, indentation and natural contour. Muscle, tendons, ligaments are all in place as part of the titanium endoskeleton."

Charlie nodded as if he knew what she was meaning. "There is no need for blood vessels or nerve endings as the whole lower leg is synthetic but there are electro receptors built in to the endoskeleton that send impulses to the brain through the connected natural tissue at the knee so the Professor can still feel. "We then encase the whole in thing in a natural skin from a compatible donor; in this case it was his son."

This made Charlie think about his plan even more and the more he thought about it, the more he was determined to succeed in saving his sons life. However, if he did save his son's life then he could not have him as a donor but this was a small price to pay, live without a leg or live without his son? There was no debate. He would go ahead with his plan and 90 years into his future, he would save his son from dying

∞

An hour later, Charlie found himself in a room like the one he was sharing with Jamie, during their stay aboard the *Blackbird*. The nurse that came out to speak to them at the hospital had advised that he relieved himself as the operation on the professor's leg would take several hours to complete. So, Ms. Stanton called for a transport platform and an assistant to take Charlie to one of the residential blocks while she stayed at the hospital.

The assistant had led Charlie through the residential block to his room, showed him how to operate the food replicator, and took her leave. Charlie was left alone again with his thoughts but not for long as Jamie came in to the room carrying a small chrome box.

Charlie's thoughts were temporarily stored away while his attention turned to his friend and the mysterious box.

"What's in there then?" he asked as Jamie carried the box over to a glass coffee table in the lounge area of the room.

"Well," Jamie said as he placed the box on the table and began to unclip the metal clasps holding the lid down. "This is our future!" and as he said this, he lifted out of the box what looked like a brown book. "It is an album," he said. "Full of pictures of our life as it will be or has been I suppose, depending on your point of view. My older self gave it to me. He said it might help us on our mission."

The boys both gathered round the table and leaned over the book as Jamie slowly opened the first page.

It was a picture of Charlie and Jamie posing for the camera smiling with an arm around each other's shoulders.

They were wearing camouflage uniforms similar to the ones they wore earlier when they went out exploring the Cretaceous period. They did not look any older than they were now but Charlie had a fresh deep cut the full length of his right cheek. They were standing in a jungle and around them were a large group of men and women all wearing the similar camouflage outfits. Something in the picture caught Charlie's eye and he studied it closer. Hanging on a gold chain around Charlie's neck was a small pendant. It seemed to be made of stone and was in the shape of a butterfly flapping its wings but before Charlie could get a closer look, Jamie innocently turned the page.

In the next picture, the boys were again standing next to each other and they were both wearing what appeared to be winter survival gear, all white and extremely padded which, was understandable considering the location they seemed to be in. All around them in the photo was white with snow and ice. There seemed to be an incredible gale blowing as well, as the pair's clothes and faces were showing signs of buffering from an icy wind.

Just visible through the fur lining of his jacket hood and under his chin, he noticed the same amulet still hanging around his neck.

"Where do you think I got that?" said Charlie pointing to the amulet.

"I don't know said Jamie but look how bloody cold we look and what's that in my hand?"

They looked at the picture again and Charlie saw in Jamie's gloved hand a canister. The same size and shape of a Thermos flask but the boys had a foreboding feeling about it and the object made them feel uneasy.

"Do you think that's the bomb?" Jamie asked.

"Well, I don't think you were dishing out cups of hot chocolate, do you?"

Jamie smiled at Charlie's attempt to lighten the mood. "No, I suppose not." He said. Jamie turned the page and they looked at the next picture.

The Charlie and Jamie in the picture were now slightly older, dressed in khakis and astride a camel each in a golden desert. Behind them were several gigantic wind turbines stretching some 300 feet up. A symbol was visible on the nearest one and it depicted two sets of outstretched wings overlapping, surrounded by a set of seven eyes. Charlie recognised it as the same set of symbols on the *Blackbirds* door.

The boys sifted through a few more pictures each with the two of them in. One depicted them climbing several hundred feet up a sheer cliff face, another picture had them in an inflatable dingy approaching an oil platform.

Charlie was particularly proud of one picture where himself and Jamie were standing on the lawn of the White House in Washington, USA and the American president was shaking Charlie's hand.

As they went through the album, there were other pictures of Charlie and Jamie with influential World leaders either shaking hands or receiving awards but Charlie stopped browsing at one particular picture.

It was a picture of Charlie but a few years older. His goatee was longer and paler in colour, his hair a little bit greyer and the cut on his cheek had healed and was replaced with a faint but distinctive scar. He was dressed in a suit and was standing in what appeared to be a study. There were rows of books on shelves in the background and a brown leather desk was directly behind him.

Charlie was not alone in the picture. Beside him on his right was a younger looking man of the same height and build. Although Charlie had obviously never met the man before, there was something strangely familiar about him.

"Who is that then?" asked Jamie, pointing to the man standing beside the older Charlie in the picture.

Charlie gazed at it for a moment and then with realisation in his voice said, "Jason. My son!"

∞

# Chapter XXII

## *The Figure*

Charlie held the album for some time unable to shake off the thought of his son dying. "I will save you," he said to himself.

Jamie put a hand on his shoulder, which brought Charlie back into the room.

"You ok mate?" Jamie asked. "You're shaking."

"I'm alright. Just a bit strange that's all," Charlie said pointing to the picture of him and his son.

"Everything is a bit strange at the moment," said Jamie. "I had a big conversation with my older self earlier and it appears that we are going straight to the jungles of South America tomorrow to rendezvous with this other ship from the 28th Century. I don't know about you but I'm getting a little bit homesick. It has been 15 hours since you fell into the underground river but I had been away for some time before I met you outside the holodeck. For me it has been weeks!"

Charlie had been so caught up with everything that he had forgotten about his own time and his family and suddenly, he felt homesick too.

"Maybe we could stop off at home before we have to go to the jungle," Charlie suggested.

"See, I said that to Professor Young," answered Jamie. "He said that time was really of the essence and any deviation from the mission would jeopardize the whole operation. Besides, he also said that he and Professor Davies did not do that in their version so I suppose we won't either."

They ate an evening meal of pizza with some rice pudding for dessert and after a couple of hours of Jamie telling Charlie all about his time travelling adventures, the boys settled down in their beds and turned out the lights.

∞

Although Charlie was exhausted after his ordeal, he had a restless disruptive sleep. Visions of velociraptors attacking his son and nuclear bombs exploding filled his mind. At one point, Charlie thought he could see a luminescent glow beyond his eyelids but when he lifted them, there was nothing but the darkness of the room. The rest of his dreams were filled with images of himself standing in a huge circular auditorium with strange looking beings all around him looking down on him from seats above. They all wore a similar pedant to the one Charlie was wearing in the pictures from earlier. All the pendants around the being's necks began to glow a luminescent blue until the light became so intense that it hurts Charlie's eyes and jolted him awake.

∞

It was morning and Charlie sat up in bed glad to be free of the tormenting and confusing nightmares. Jamie was in the shower and Charlie could hear him singing through the door.

Charlie pulled back the covers of his bed, stood up and walked over to the window that covered most of the wall opposite the room's main entrance.

Taking a satisfying stretch Charlie pressed the button, at the side of the full-length curtains, which said open, and the curtains began to slide sideways away from each other.

What was revealed to Charlie as the curtains parted, was breath taking.

An artificial sun had been created for the station and Charlie and Jamie's room faced east. As he gazed out of the window at the towering buildings, Charlie could feel his face warm as the sun rose up above the lower buildings. When it cleared the final, one the light was blinding and Charlie had to shield his eyes until they adjusted to the glare. The sun reflected off the taller structures creating several straight rainbows as the buildings acted like prisms.

There was a knock at the door and after Charlie called "come in" the main door opened and an assistant came in with a hover table of different items of clothing and objects.

"Good morning sir, she said. Hope you are well this morning?        Professor Young will be up to see you in one hour and Professor Davies wishes you to know that his operation was a success and he should be able to join you in the briefing room later.

"In the meantime, we have prepared the personal equipment that you will need for your journey. Please get yourself dressed and after breakfast ring the bell and I will come and get you."

The assistant left and Charlie went over to the hover table. On it he found two sets of combat overalls with boots the same as the ones he and Jamie were wearing in the first photo they looked at. Charlie rummaged through the rest of the stuff on the table but it was not the utility belt full of medicines, the torch, or the survival knife lying in its sheath that interested him. What he was looking for was not there; the pendant that he saw himself wearing in the pictures. Where did it come from?

∞

When Jamie came out of the shower, Charlie had one and once he was dried and dressed, the two of them sat and ate their breakfast.

"So, this is it", said Jamie. "This is the first day of our destiny. Do you think we can do this, I mean the mission?"

"I don't know," said Charlie, "but we have to. Our future depends on it. I always thought that we were put on the planet for some purpose but who would have thought that it would be to save it!"

When they had finished their breakfast, they rang the bell next to the door and the assistant came to accompany them to the briefing room. The two boys followed the assistant out of their room, along the corridors to a waiting transport platform that carried them off to Control.

As the boys glided away from the walkway, a cloaked figure stepped out of the shadow of a doorway and watched the transport disappear around one of the tall-mirrored buildings.

"Do you think he will succeed?" The figure said.

Another figure joined the first. "He must," It said. The fate of all of us rests in his hands, especially mine!"

As the cloaked figure turned to look at his companion, it held out an object for the other figure to take. "This will help him on his quest. He may only use it once and only he can decide whom to save."

The other figure took the object from the cloaked figure and watched as it retracted a grey, thin, three fingered hand back into the dark folds of its cloaks sleeve. It then retreated back into the shadows leaving the second figure alone.

"I will do everything in my power to help you," he said to the now disappeared transport platform, "even if it means the ultimate sacrifice!"

Jason turned away from where his father had just left on the transport platform, and walked into a waiting turbo-lift.

∞

# Chapter XXIII

## *The Fan*

When they arrived at the briefing room, Charlie and Jamie found the older selves and Commander Cunningham already there to meet them. As they entered, both the professors stood up to greet them. Charlie particularly noticed how fresh and alert his older self looked.

"How do you like the new leg?" Professor Davies asked.

They could not see it because of the combat trousers he was wearing but the professor stood up to his full height and just his presence commanded respect and admiration.

"Shall we get down to business then? he said as they all sat down at the table.

Ms. Stanton and Admiral Aziz had joined them, found their seats just as Professor Davies spoke again.

"Today is an historic day in more ways than one. Today we embark on a mission that will either change the course of time or hopefully, keep it the same!"

Commander Cunningham stood up and asked for people's attention to be drawn to a holographic map that had appeared suspended above the table.

The map was of South America and as they watched, it expanded as a red dot appeared and grew larger as the map homed in on the point.

"Jump time is at 14:00 our time. An AZ has been selected as close to the co-ordinates of the *Avocet* as possible."

"I am assuming that the *Avocet* is this other ship from the future?" asked Jamie.

"Yes," replied the commander. Due to the now constantly changing time field and the historical shifting of the tectonic plates, the closest we can get to it is within 10 miles of the rendezvous point, which means, we will have to go out on foot once we arrive. The habitat is quite hostile being dense rainforest all around otherwise we would have taken the hover skis.

"Professors Davies and Young know the general direction we need to head in once we land which should take us straight to the ship."

"In our defence," said Professor Young, "it was 90 years ago and we had a lot on our minds at the time."

"Don't we know it!" said Jamie.

"Once we reach the *Avocet*," Commander Cunningham continued, "we can radio for the *Blackbird* to come and pick us up.

"We will then head straight down to the Antarctic and plant the charge that we picked up from the *Avocet*."

The holographic map changed in front of them to a 3D image of the Antarctic continent. A red dot appeared in the centre of the hologram.

Commander Cunningham using a laser pen highlighted the area. "We have calculated that this is where the charge needs to be placed. It is an extinct volcanic vent that when the bomb goes off, will act as a funnel and eject the compound out at a force four times greater than the nuclear charge alone would create. It will have a similar effect to that of a bullet being fired out of the barrel of a gun."

"How deep is this vent?" Charlie asked.

Professor Young stood up and walked across the room to a large white board. He picked up a felt pen and began to draw a diagram of the vent on the board. "The professor and I measured it at 200 meters down and at a 20° angle. The shaft of the vent was 10 meters across and because of the angle; it could only take one man at a time."

Out the corner of his eye, Charlie noticed his older self seemed to deflate in response to what Professor Young had said. The older man's shoulders sagged and his head bowed for a moment then he looked up and there was a visible sadness in his eyes.

Professor Young continued. "We will only have a short space of time to send someone down the shaft, plant the bomb, then evacuate the area to a safe distance before the bomb detonates."

"How short?" asked Charlie.

"The bomb has a 60-minute fuse and unfortunately, we cannot deviate from that window due to the rapidly changing time patterns."

"One hour until Jump time for Discovery Cruiser *Blackbird*" came an announcement of the tannoy.

"Ok gentlemen, please finalise all preparations and deliver all equipment to Jakes and his team down in the storage bays. Needles can show you where to go," spoke up Professor Davies. Charlie noticed the sadness he had seen before, had lifted and once again, the commanding, authoritative voice was back in Professor Davies.

They all stood up and Charlie and Jamie followed Commander Cunningham out of the room into a turbo lift while the others stayed behind.

"I took the liberty of sending for your things from your room and have them sent down to the loading bays," Needles said. "There is also a change of clothes for you both and a side arm allocated to each of you. All that is needed is your finger prints to register the firearm to you personally."

"A gun?" exclaimed Jamie.

"Just a precautionary measure," explained the commander. "Self defence in case things get...messy!"

The three of them exited the lift when it finally came to a halt at sub level. The *Blackbird* stood before them in a vast artificial cavern. Various figures busied themselves around the ship, crawling over it like ants. Checking solar cells or adjusting ion casings. Small hover trucks zipped back and forth, carrying silver boxes into the ships storage decks and one pulled up alongside the three men.

"The weapons that you requested, Sir," said the driver, and handed the Commander two small silver brief cases. "Also, I have the gentlemen's clothing."

"Thank you, corporal. Here we are gentlemen," and Needles opened the small silver brief cases. "Take them," he said. "They will immediately be registered to your individual palm print so nobody else can use them."

Charlie and Jamie reached out and each took a small, black pistol that had been resting in its foam packaged case. As soon as they held them firmly in their hands, the guns emitted a digital beep and a computerized voice stated "New user recognised. Individual palm recognition verification required, processing data." There was another beep and after a second or two, a red light on the side of each gun blinked to green. "Palm recognition verified," the voice said. "Welcome Professor Davies, Professor Young," the two guns said in unison.

"Our technology in this time recognises you both but as your older selves," smiled the commander when he saw the boys confused faces. "Your unique finger prints and patterns on your hands do not change over time even if the rest of you does."

The two boys placed their pistols back in their cases and closed the lids.

They followed the commander further into the loading bay as he checked off lists on clipboards and barked orders to those running to and fro with various boxes, canisters, and bags.

"Sir", came a voice as a young man, not much older than the two boys, perhaps no more than eighteen came running up to the trio.

"What is it ensign?" asked Commander Cunningham.

At the sight of Charlie and Jamie, the man stopped, mouth wide open, staring at them. After a few seconds he eventually seemed to snap out of his trance. "Erm...Sergeant Jakes has asked if you could come and finalise the loading of the polar equipment into Bay 23?"

"Of course," said the commander. "I'll be right there. Gentlemen, if you would excuse me? Billy here will escort you up to your quarters. I will see you in 40 minutes on the observation deck for jump time." And with that, the commander turned and left the three men alone.

"I am a huge fan of you guys!" said Billy as soon as the commander was out of earshot. "I have read all your books and studied all of your jumps. You are living legends! The work you have done has made this society today and our way of life better than ever!" He shook both their hands enthusiastically. "I want to be just like you when I'm older."

This statement seemed to amuse Jamie who let out a loud laugh. "We're younger than you!" he coughed.

"I know," said Billy "but you will become such great men. Your work will shape the world. If it wasn't for you two, many of us wouldn't be where we are today. Commander Cunningham has followed in your footsteps and is one of the sincerest and devoted to the cause people that I know! You," and here he pointed to Jamie, "picked me up from the gutter and gave me the chance to be someone, to make a difference. You said, no matter how small an action, you can make the biggest of changes."

Jamie turned to Charlie. "Well, it's true, isn't it?!" He said teasingly.

They entered a turbo-lift and Billy took them up to Level E and to their room.

"It has been a pleasure speaking with you, gentleman," Billy exclaimed shaking them both very firmly by the hand. With one last admiring look, he turned and disappeared down the corridor.

"Speaking *with?*" laughed Jamie. Rather more speaking *to*! He wouldn't stop talking all the way up in the lift. He's worse than me!"

Charlie wasn't listening. He had found his way over to the photo album they had been looking at earlier. The pendant seemed to be calling to him from the pictures and he had an irresistible urge to confront his older self and ask about it.

However, before he had time to pluck up the courage, reach for the intercom and call the professor, an announcement stated they had "twenty minutes before jump time."

"We'd better get dressed and head to the Obs deck", said Jamie.

Charlie closed the book he had been looking at and began to change into the outdoor combat gear he wore for their first exploration. Although less than 24 hours had passed since he arrived on the ship, Charlie was starting to feel part of this new world, his future, and although he was right in the middle of an unimaginable adventure, a foreboding feeling hung over everything and Charlie knew that the adventure couldn't last.

∞

# Chapter XXIV

## *The Jungle*

Charlie and Jamie arrived on the observation deck fifteen minutes later dressed in the same camouflage outfits they wore before but this time they had their new handguns in holsters strapped to their legs.

"Welcome gentlemen," announced Professor Davies as the two boys sat down at the round table in the middle of the room.

Professor Young was also present alongside Commander Cunningham, Admiral Aziz, Captain Jeffreys, and Ms. Stanton.

"Are you ready?" the professor asked.

"Not really, no" replied Charlie, "but do I have a choice?"

"Not really, no", his older self replied. "I am sorry but it has to be this way."

The rumble of the six massive Time Quantum Engines drowned out any reply Charlie was thinking of giving as the *Blackbird* roared to life, lifting off its landing gear, gently gliding out of the landing bay doors where it had settled the previous day, and floated out into space.

"Engage TQE's to Jump level in 30 seconds," voiced the commander into a microphone. "All crew prepare for Jump. Gentlemen, Madam, please fasten your safety belts." The commander sat down while a voice began the ten second countdown.

"Here we go again," smiled Jamie but Charlie was far from feeling humorous. This was it, he thought. In less than ten seconds he would be hurtling through time to meet his destiny. The future had placed the responsibility on him to save the planet from an environmental disaster but all he could think about was how he could save his son. At what stage would he meet him? Would he be able to alter the course of the future or will his son's fate also be sealed along with the fate on billions? Time would tell but Charlie had very little time left and it was quickly running out.

"Mark!" The voice over the tannoy announced as the cacophony from the engines reached its peak and the now familiar streaking of stars began to form outside the observation window.

*Lewis Davies*

A final clap like thunder signaled the *Blackbird*s departure as the space station continued to gently spin in space.

∞

From the air, the jungles of South America were a beautiful carpet of green shrouded in a blanket of mist, from ground level the twisted vines, almost impassable brush, and the sinking, shifting ground under foot made the jungle the worst place to be.

The exploration team had landed five hours previous and should have covered the 10 miles to the estimated rendezvous point but due to the toughness of the terrain they had only travelled just half the distance.

Their journey in the jungle had been relatively uneventful with only a small incident involving a tapir uncharacteristically charging one of the team and breaking their arm. Equipment was abandoned and the soldier injured made their way back to *Blackbird,* unable to take part in the remainder of the expedition.

Eventually a halt had to be made for the close of day and the ground team began clearing an area to set up camp.

Charlie and Jamie helped build a large fire in the centre while tents and a perimeter security fence were erected.

After two hours, the area was secured and the team was settling down for the night.

Charlie and Jamie sat next to the fire drinking cocoa while the team shared stories of past missions. Spirits were high and all around the camp there was an air of confidence in the mission. Laughter echoed off the trees and the team felt like they could save the world!

One person though, did not seem to be enjoying the revelries and he got up from the fire and walked away from the light in to the dark of the night. Jamie noticed his older self leave and got up to follow. Charlie didn't notice his friend was absent. He was too busy listening to one of the soldier's talking about a trip to the 22nd Century to relocate Blue Whales. Even he was feeling confident and thoughts of his son temporarily were forgotten in the lightness of the mood.

Jamie circled the camp fire to where his older self had been sitting and stepped out of the glowing circle. He found the professor sitting in his tent, head bowed looking through a photo album similar to the one Charlie and Jamie had sifted through the day before.

The professor spoke without lifting his head as Jamie gently entered the tent. "The world is changing, Jamie. Time is running out for all of us." Professor Young finally slowly raised his head and looked at Jamie. There were tears in his eyes and his face was pale. "Would you give up everything for Charlie if you had too?" he asked.

"Of course,", Jamie said instantly. There was confusion over his face.

"Do not be so hasty to answer so definite," his older self snapped. "A question like that needs thought, it needs consideration, it needs time for you to seriously think about your answer before you jump in and give such a frivolous response!"

Jamie reeled at this explosive retort and a slight hint of fear but also defensiveness was in his voice when he next spoke would.

"I *would* give up everything for Charlie!" he retaliated. He is the closest friend I have ever had and I feel that I ever will. We have known each other since we were three years old. We have grown up together, inseparable through the good and the bad times. Yes, we argue but that just strengthens the bond between us. I love him wholeheartedly and would be half the person I am today without him. He is my brother and I would die for him!"

Jamie stood there for a moment until he realised that he was breathing heavily and his fists were clenched. He forced himself to relax and awaited another barrage from the professor in response to his own tirade but nothing came.

Instead the professor sat looking at him. A look of serenity had crossed his face and it seemed as if the professor had made up his mind about something. "That," he finally said "is a worthy answer. There are many answers to simple questions that most people throw around so nonchalantly that they do not truly understand their own meaning. To really answer a question, you must accept that the response you give, is really what you want to say."

Jamie looked at the professor confused. "I do not understand," he said.

The professor smiled. "Not everything spoken is understood at the time it is said," he replied. "We just need to accept that whether it is a spoken word or an action, everything is preset and is part of the cycle of things. Time is unstoppable and passes along a predetermined path. It is that which travels on that path that cannot be avoided and has already become part of history before it has happened. Your future and mine has been written and we need to accept our fate.

"You say that you would give up your life for Charlie?" Jamie nodded.

The professor paused for a moment as if rehearsing his next words. Jamie half expected another cryptic speech about fate and future but eventually, all the professor finally said was, "so would I!"

∞

Jamie stepped outside the tent confused and scared. His older self seemed saddened as if he was in mourning but there was also a hint of acceptance in his voice. Jamie had left the professor still sitting looking at the photo album. He had noticed that the professor had the album open at a copy of the same picture Charlie and he had been looking at the day before. The picture of the two of them not much older than they were now, dressed in the same camouflage gear, they were now wearing in the jungle.

"Where have you been?" piped up Charlie as Jamie wondered into their own tent. The revelry around the camp fire had died down on the orders of Professor Davies reasoning they had an early start the next day to reach the *Avocet* before noon.

"Talking to myself," Jamie replied but Charlie could not get any more out of him and they both settled down into their sleeping bags and the lights dimmed around the camp.

∞

# Chapter XXV

## *The Attack*

It was still dark when the two boys were roughly shaken awake by one of the soldiers from the ground team.

"We are being attacked!" he cried and ran back out of the tent.

Charlie and Jamie immediately leapt out of their sleeping bags, grabbed their holstered weapons that instantly sprang to life at their touch and raced out of their tent. What greeted them when they stepped outside was carnage.

The camp was in chaos. Figures were running back and forth in the darkness and all around, were the sounds of screams and the zip zip of laser fire from pulsar rifles.

It was hard to see what was going on as the only light was the thin white beams from torches as they crisscrossed across the arena.

A soldier, dressed from only the waste down, his upper body spattered with blood, careered into the two boys standing gaping at the scene in front of them. The doomed man fell to the ground at their feet, gasping his last breaths of life.

Charlie knelt and cradled the dying man's head in his arms.   There   was   a short spear of perhaps only two-foot-long embedded in his chest. His face, body and arms were covered in deep gashes from where he openly bled.

"What happened?" whispered Charlie.

The soldier slowly opened his eyes. "They came at us from the shadows," he coughed, blood trickling from his mouth and down his chin. "They took us by surprise!"

"Who?" asked Charlie. "Who took you by surprise?" but the man was already dead before Charlie could finish his question. Gently lying the man's head down on the ground, Charlie stood back up and surveyed the scene again.

Through the smoke created by expended plasma rounds, the boys could make out a number of bodies lying around the now extinct fire. Several soldiers lay still, short spears sticking out of them but a few corpses strewn about were what appeared to be children. Small figures half the size of an average adult human being and wearing nothing but dark cloth around their waists that hung to just above the knee. Their bodies were black skinned and a thick dark carpet of hair covered their arms, legs, head and torso.

Charlie stepped forward to examine one closer. Suddenly, before he knew what had happened, he felt a huge blow to his left side and he fell to the ground. Instantly, a creature was on top of him growling and screaming. Charlie managed to focus and saw it was one of the small figures he saw lying motionless but this was one was very much alive.

It was human in face but had a burning hatred behind the eyes. It drooled and spat as it tried to bite at Charlie's face with sharp, pointed teeth. When he had been knocked over, Charlie instinctively had raised his hands to protect his face. This action had saved him from more serious injury, as his attacker had managed to scratch a long gash into Charlie's cheek using a sharpened animal bone. Now it was held at bay by Charlie managing to slowly push back.

The creature lay on top of him and was kicking and clawing trying to get the upper hand and kill the young boy it was on top of.

Charlie began to slowly push his hands up, lifting his attacker away from his face until he had managed to lock his elbows and straighten his arms. The small creature continued to struggle, still trying to reach Charlie's face but Charlie now had the creature at arm's length and the small beast was almost suspended in midair with its arms and legs flailing wildly.

Suddenly a bright bolt of light hit the creature in the side of the head and sent it stumbling off Charlie's outstretched arms. It fell to the ground dead, a large hole in its head and its brain splattered down what was left of its face.

Charlie turned to his left to see Jamie slowly lowering his pistol, smoke dissipating from the barrel.

"Thanks mate," he said with a relieved smile.

"No problem!" Jamie replied, somewhat a little shaken up. Suddenly again, he lifted his pistol and fired off a pulsar round at a figure to their right.

The solider, the fallen creature was chasing waved a hand of gratitude and ran on, firing his own rifle into the darkness. "I think I'm getting the hang of this," quivered Jamie.

Charlie un-holstered his pistol and they were just about to enter the fray when a blinding light filled the whole camp and the boys felt a burning sensation rip through their entire bodies. They both collapsed to the ground and fell in to unconsciousness.

∞

When Charlie awoke, he found himself lying where he fell and Jamie beside him. Hands gently gripped his arms lifting him up and helped him to stand. As his focus became clear, he saw the familiar face of his older self staring at him, a look of relief on his face.

"You alright?" he said.

"What happened?" Charlie finally said after a drink of water from a bottle handed to him from one of the various figures now standing around him. Jamie was being helped up next to him and the camp, although it seemed destroyed was bright and calm again.

"We were attacked," the professor quietly said. "By a particularly vicious race of pygmies." The professor continued as Charlie and Jamie tried to come to terms with what he had just said.

"They had been following us since we landed but waited until nightfall to launch their attack. They took out our perimeter guards first with poison darts, and then launched a full-scale charge. Many our men were cut down in the first wave of attack but we turned the tables when the second wave hit. Their spears and knives were no match for our pulsar rifles and we managed to drive them back but their numbers were vast and more and more came. If it wasn't for the team from the *Avocet*, we would all be dead."

"They're here?" gasped Charlie.

"No," answered the professor. "But they picked up our pulsar relays from our weapons on their scanners and locked on to our location. They launched a seismic electrical charge into the area covering a one-mile radius. The charge renders all life-forms with a carbon level of more than 100, unconscious, namely, you and the pygmies."

"So why did it not affect you?" asked Jamie.

"All the work that that the EGU has undertaken over the centuries has helped to reduce carbon emissions and create a better quality of ozone. In the 24th Century, the levels of carbon in the atmosphere has been reduced to only 2.5 grams per 100 square feet. This is a 75% reduction of the levels that occurred in 2010. We hadn't managed to reduce the levels of carbon in the air significantly and air pollution was still a major issue for the era.

"In time the air quality improved and EGU's work continued to influence the reduction in carbon emissions until, by the late 21st Century, people had healthier lungs and air to breath, hence why were not affected by the electric pulse."

"I still don't understand," said Jamie. "So, how were we affected?"

"A little-known fact is that carbon has a small electrical charge," continued the professor. "We all have small amounts of carbon in our bodies hence 'carbon life-forms', and sometimes that carbon will emit an electrical charge, whether you have felt it when brushing passed metal or shaking someone's hand. You may have felt a small shock from the contact. This is because there has been an excess buildup of carbon and it needs to be released. You two were affected by the pulse because you have high levels of carbon in your bodies and the electrical pulse induced the expulsion of an excess amount of carbon based electrical charge. The large levels of carbon created a large electric shock which was enough to shut down your consciousness without suppressing your vital organs functions."

"Oh, well that makes sense," jibed Jamie.

"It also explains why the attacking pygmies were all incapacitated too," followed Charlie.

The professor nodded while a medic saw to Charlie's cut on his cheek. It was a deep 6-inch gash running the length of his cheek and the medic administered several stitches while Charlie asked another question.

"What have you done with the pygmies?"

At that point Sergeant Patrick came running up and whispered in Professor Davies' ear. The professor turned and began to stare at Jamie and, while still listening to the sergeant, slowly nodded in agreement at something the sergeant had said.

"The pygmies have been 'taken care of'" he said. "Jamie, I need you to come with me!"

The professor slowly turned beckoning for Jamie to follow. Jamie did so and as he walked past Sergeant Patrick, the soldier put his arm over Jamie's shoulder and guided him gently away from Charlie and the team gathered around.

∞

Jamie followed the professor through the camp until they finally came to the edge of the boundary. In a section of the clearing was a large knotted old tree stump. A remnant of a once enormous tree, the trunk now lay a few feet away where it had fallen and snapped decades ago.

Leaning slumped against the log with a spear sticking out of his stomach and his left arm severed below the elbow was Professor Young.

Jamie immediately rushed to his side and tried to grasp sanity of the situation.

"Get a medic!" he screamed. "Please, help me stop the bleeding!" Jamie struggled to fight back the tears as he attempted to bandage his older self's wounds with torn pieces of cloth from his t-shirt.

Nobody came to his aid. The two men stood there with tears in their eyes, watching the young boy frivolously attempt to stop the inevitable.

"Why won't you help?" Jamie cried.

"It is too late," Professor Davies confessed. "For us this has already happened. We have already seen this day and prepared for it."

Jamie looked upon the face of his older self and saw a subtle smile form on the weary face.

"Do not be sad," the professor gasped. "This is meant to be. We have always known I would meet my end tonight. We have had a good life, you and me. We have seen some incredible things and we have been part of an amazing adventure that has changed the universe. Do not grieve for me. Be strong, for you need to be as determined and focused as you will ever be if Charlie is to succeed."

At these words, Charlie came into the clearing and looked upon the sad scene before him.

Jamie was openly weeping now as he cradled the dying professor in his arms.

The professor choked on some rising blood in his throat but managed to continue to speak. "I do not have long now," he whispered. "Remember this night and never forget that everything has been set. Our past cannot be completely changed but influenced in subtle ways to slightly alter the future. My death has been written but cannot be altered. Life and death are the exceptions to the rule and will never be controlled. I have embraced this fact and accept my death openly. It is how it influences people's actions in the future that we decide everything."

The professor closed his eyes and gave out a long gurgling gasp. "Focus... on... the... future..., Jamie." He managed to utter. "Your... decisions... will... change... the... World!" and with that, Professor Young died. Jamie bowed his head and gently lay his older self down on the ground.

Everyone in the clearing bowed their heads except one. Professor Davies was intently looking at Charlie, a single tear rolled down his cheek. His younger self did not notice. Charlie was staring at his grieving friend. If only they had known this was to happen. Why couldn't their older selves have avoided it? Why did they allow Professor Young to die? Yes, they said that life and death are set and cannot be avoided but surely if you know it will happen, then you can prevent it?

Charlie could not accept that he would not be able to save his son and as everyone stood around mourning the loss of their friend, he felt even more confident and determined than ever that he would not let Jason befall the same fate as Professor Young.

Professor Davies looked on from across the clearing and with what seemed a great sadness, gently shook his head.

∞

# Chapter XXVI

## *The Loss*

They buried the professor where he lay, piling rocks around his body and erecting a small wooden cross on the top of the cairn. On the front of the pile of stones lay a piece of bark that Jamie had etched a short epitaph.

*"Here lies Professor Jamie Young. Remembered*
*For all of Time"*

*Lewis Davies*

He also laid his zippo lighter next to the plaque while it seemed as if the whole forest lay silent with not even a bird revealing its presence.

After what seemed an eternity, the crowd gathered, slowly dispersed, Professor Davies among them, leaving Jamie and Charlie next to the grave.

After a moment of silence, Jamie spoke, the sound of grief and remorse clearly in his voice.

"They could have saved him," he gently said. "He could have avoided last night, be anywhere else but here! Why didn't he? Why didn't he just stay away?" Jamie began crying again and Charlie placed an empathetic hand on his shoulder. He tried to find words of comfort, something he could say to justify his own selfish thoughts of Jason but no words came out. Instead, Charlie stood there, not moving. He could not tell Jamie what he was planning to do. He could not tell anybody, not even his older self. The professor would most certainly lecture him that it was not possible to prevent the inevitable and that Jason must die in the velociraptor attack. It was written.

As the two boys stood alone in their grief, Professor Davies watched them from the dark. "It cannot be avoided, Charlie," he thought to himself. "Jason will give the ultimate sacrifice for the both of us and we cannot change that! Stay strong. You will soon understand." He wiped away the tears that were now running down his face and turned away from the boys and headed back to the camp.

∞

Charlie and Jamie eventually retired to their tent and both fell into a disturbed sleep. Charlie's dreams, again were dominated by images of tall hooded figures staring down at him from above as he stood in a large arena. The amulets around their necks began to glow brighter and brighter to the point where Charlie's eyes felt like they were burning. Suddenly, the light disappeared and he found himself face down in a sloping tunnel, his hand reaching out into the dark as he felt himself being pulled back. He screamed out as if he was calling to someone down the tunnel but no sound came out. A huge jolt took him backwards and a blinding explosion juddered him awake.

Charlie found himself lying in his sleeping bag in his tent. Jamie gently snored beside him and through the gap in the door, the first rays of the dawn began to seep in to the tent. Charlie climbed out of his sleeping bag and crawled out of the tent.

The carnage from the night before was evident in the growing light. Several broken tents were strewn across the camp while boxes of equipment and their contents were scattered across the area. The ground was stained with dried blood and the bodies of pygmies still lay where they were slain.

A few of the team were also up and were salvaging as much equipment and supplies as they could. The members of the expedition who had fallen in the battle the night before had been removed from camp and had been shown the same respect as Professor Young.

Charlie weaved his way through the devastation not sure where he was going. His head was whirl of confusion and the more he tried to remember his dream, the more the memory slipped away until eventually, all that he could recollect was the moment he was staring down a tunnel, reaching out to an unknown voice in the darkness. This filled Charlie with a confusion of grief of which, he had no idea of its source. What would make him feel so helpless, so empty inside?

His thoughts were interrupted by Professor Davies gently taking him by the shoulders. Charlie looked up to see the warm face of his older self looking at him.

"I feel your grief," he said. "Although mine is 90 years older, it is no less. Professor Young...," Charlie's older self hesitated, "...Jamie," he continued "was my friend for over a century and I will miss him more than I can say. We have known all too well for decades that the events of last night were to pass which made it even more difficult to allow it to happen."

"Then why did you?" asked Charlie in an angry voice. "Why did you let Professor Young die when you could have saved him? What is the good of foresight if you do not use it?"

The professor pondered this for a moment and when he next spoke, again there was the sadness in his voice that Charlie had heard before.

"My role in this mission," he said "is of greater importance than Professor Young's was. Last night Professor Young saved me from a fatal attack by stepping in front of a spear that had been aimed at my heart. Knowing he was to die, he made the ultimate sacrifice for me so I would continue with the mission. I still have a part to play and if Jamie had not intervened, the mission would fail. We had always known that Jamie would die here, now, in this jungle, during an attack. We had witnessed it all as you have now, as young men 90 years ago, we were just unsure in what capacity it would happen. All we had were the memories of you and young Jamie witnessing everything you have up until now."

Charlie tried to absorb everything he was hearing. "But, if you knew you were going to be attacked and Jamie would die protecting you, then why did you not just avoid the battle?"

"As I have already told you," answered the professor in a calm voice, "we did not know precisely when it was going to happen last night so we could not avoid it. Birth and death, are the only two things that are sureties. They cannot be avoided or altered. They are set in time and are not susceptible to these rips in the timeline that we are experiencing.

"But surely you could now tell me when and where it happened last night?" answered Charlie. I could then carry that information with me for 90 years and prevent Jamie being killed?"

"It has already happened though," interjected the professor. "If you did indeed use the information you now have to prevent Jamie's death then this conversation will never need to have happened. However, then you would not have received the information of Jamie's death and you would not be in a position to prevent it. It is a paradoxical equation that cannot be altered. It deeply saddens me to say but Jamie's death last night was inevitable and you cannot prevent someone from dying."

There was a strong emphasis on the last six words and it seemed the tone of the professor's voice was enough to tell Charlie that that particular conversation was over.

∞

After two hours of packing and clearing up, the team were ready to continue their journey towards the *Phoenix*.

The rest of the trip was a quiet one. Not only through lack of event but the team were silent, locked in their own individual thoughts after the previous night. None more so than Jamie, who, it seemed, had retreated into himself and would not let anyone in. Charlie tried on various occasions to communicate with him but he did not appear to notice or hear his friend as they slowly hacked their way through the dense forest.

The heat and humidity had reached an intolerable intensity when they finally came to halt besides a welcoming fast flowing stream that wound its way through the trees. After filling their cantinas and bathing their tired feet, they set off back into the jungle with even less determination than before.

After 2 more hours cutting through the unrelenting thick vegetation, morale was low and confidence in ever reaching their destination had been all but sapped from every member of the expedition until suddenly, a cry up ahead from one of the head scouts, broke the white noise of the forest and lifted their spirits. 7 hours after leaving camp, they had finally reached the *Phoenix*.

∞

# Chapter XXVII

## *The Meeting*

The ship was hardly visible through the thick vegetation that now covered almost the entirety of the hull. Vines crawled across its stained, white exterior and trees, over decades of succession, had rooted themselves to the top of the ship and were now fighting to gain height and gather the vital rays of sun that broke through the canopy above.

It looked like a huge mound of growth with every inch of the ship being covered with vines, ferns, trees, shrubs, and grasses. Leaf litter gathered in the crevices while pools of green stagnant water had formed in and around the windows, vents, and ducts of the ship.

The only section that did not have growth was a small 3-metre-wide clearing at the left-hand side. The area seemed to have been cleared and kept free of vegetation while the rest of the ship had succumbed to the forest.

As the team approached, an electronic whirring noise began to crescendo and from the thicket of vines and branches, a long metal ramp descended at an angle toward the ground and came to rest in the clearing.

A pale blue light like the one Charlie saw emanate from the medallions in his dream, now flooded the clearing in an alien glow that made the surrounding forest look eerie and disturbingly dangerous.

Figures began to descend the ramp and their shadows pierced the light, casting long silhouettes on the ramp and the ground.

As Charlie watched, hooded figures appeared from the ship. They were similarly dressed to the ones that he had seen during the attack on the camp the night before. The figures approached the team and finally stood before them. The lead figure reached up with grey 3 fingered hands, and slid the hood off its head and the rest of the figures followed suit.

Charlie saw clearly for the first time the alien creatures that had helped them at the camp and had haunted his dreams for the past few nights.

They were tall, thin and their skin was grey-blue and smooth. Their heads were large and oval shaped with no facial features to speak of apart from a small thin mouth and two large lidless, pupil-less eyes.

What seemed to be the leader spoke. "Welcome to the *Avocet*," he said, and held out a hand to greet Professor Davies who had stepped forward.

"Good to see you again Dorak", the professor said with a smile. "I am sorry it has taken so long!"

"It could not be helped", replied the alien in a metallic sounding voice. "This moment and all that has come before it has been foreseen. We have been devoted to waiting and seeing that this meeting would occur. All that we know or will be, relies on this mission succeeding. Myself and my team are committed to our part of fate and all our destiny."

"Where is my son?" the professor asked.

At this shocking statement, Charlie gasped in confusion. What? Was his son here? Was he going to meet him already?

It was true that his elder self had not said when his son died only how.

Could it be that he could warn him in advance about the raptor attack?

Charlie followed as both groups headed toward the access ramp tucked amongst the thickets of vegetation.

He was going to meet his son? It was almost too much for Charlie to take in and he began to feel weak, stumbling up the ramp.

For the first time since leaving the camp, Jamie showed signs of awareness. "You ok? He asked, catching Charlie before he could fall.

"I'm alright," Charlie replied. "I just can't believe I'm going to meet my son!"

They were the last to enter the ship and as they did, the ramp raised behind them and whirred shut.

They found themselves in a brightly lit corridor of similar design to the *Blackbird* and followed everyone else down it to a large meeting room with an oval table in the centre.

Standing behind a chair, with his hands on the back of it and facing the door was the man Charlie had seen in the photos back at Control. His son, Jason!

As the group entered the room Jason came from behind the chair and embraced his father. It was a long embrace and one that reflected the extreme length of time apart. Charlie noticed though that there was more to greeting each other, there was something intensely definitive about it. As if it was the last time they would ever have the opportunity to be happy together again.

As they embraced, the professor whispered to his son. "I am so sorry I took so long to get here!"

Jason softly smiled at his father. "It's ok, Dad," he said kindly. "We both know why it has to happen this way, why I had to go into the future to call on Dorak and his team."

The professor held his son tighter until finally, he seemed to accept the situation for what it was and loosened his grip. "The future of the world is reliant on just the few of us," he whispered. "I love you Jason and I am so very proud of you." He gave his son one final lasting embrace, then released him and turned away to talk to Dorak.

Charlie felt overwhelmed to see his future son and was eager to get him alone to discuss his plan to save him. The professor and Jason unlocked and turned to Charlie standing patiently.

"This is Jason, my son," the professor said with a tear in his eye.

Charlie took Jason's hand as Jason said with a smile. "It is good to finally meet you, as it were!"

"This is strange!" Charlie said. "You are older than me but yet, I am your father!"

"I know!" Jason replied. "Ever since Dad told me that I was going to meet you here, on this day, I have been wondering what I would say to you. I asked him what we spoke about when we met as he can remember today from when he was you, but, he would not divulge any more information than the fact we talked a lot!"

Charlie leaned in closer as the rest of the group took up seats around the table. "I have to tell you something," he whispered, "but it will have to wait until later."

*Lewis Davies*

Jason nodded in agreement but he had an innocent look of confusion on his face.

The two men turned and took their seats at the table as the alien, Dorak stood at the head and began to speak.

∞

"Friends," he began. "We have reached a crossroads in all our times. A crossroads that has only one direction, but if we lose our way, it will create a future that none of will ever be able to return to. We are part of a changing present and the time before us will mould around this reality leaving us trapped on an alternative time line to our own. Our mission must succeed or all will be lost.

"For some of us, the events that are to pass are already part of our history. We remember this moment and we remember the mission because we lived it and we succeeded. However, the crack in the timeline has shifted more than we calculated and now every chapter in history may be re-written. A time loop has formed which will find this moment being repeated over and over."

*Lewis Davies*

Dorak pointed to Charlie with a long grey finger. "You will grow up to be the great man you see before you." He motioned to the professor. "In the future you will meet yourself as you are now and replay the last few days all over again and again and again but only if you succeed again and again and again. This is inevitable and can never be allowed to stop, no matter how painful events may be. On each re-enactment, the crack is distorting time and unless the mission is played out exactly each time, with no diversion, then the mission will not succeed and a time paradox will cause the collapse of the entire universe."

There was a general murmur of agreement around the table but Charlie was silent. His mind was racing at the thought that even if they deviated from the mission for a moment, then that would be it. Game over!        But as Charlie tried to digest and understand everything Dorak had just said, it occurred to him that Jason's death and the raptor attack occurred after this mission. When he first met his older self in the 24$^{th}$ century only a few days ago, the professor and his team had only just returned from the fateful mission where Jason lost his life. This meant that Charlie had decades to prepare and it would have absolutely no effect on the mission now.

With this new revelation, Charlie felt himself grow in confidence, his determination now aimed at completing the mission. If the fate of all was in his hands, then he was not going to disappoint. Jason could wait and a sudden surge of adrenaline coursed through his body.

To everyone's surprise, most of all, his own, he stood up to everyone address the room.

"Three days ago, I was a simple boy with simple interests living a simple life in a simple world. I have since discovered that time travel is not restricted to fiction books, aliens do exist, and I grow up to be one of the saviours of the universe! That is a lot to take in, in three days.

"If I felt anyone was not up for the job, it was me. I don't know much about science or technology," he added, "and my head is struggling to keep up with the complications of time travel, but what I do know, is I will do everything I can to see this through. If it is written that my role in all this is a significant one, then so be it. Many people live their lives day by day, never really making an impression or having any relevance. We only have a short life (mostly) but it is what we do with it that counts. I do not know what lies ahead, or what challenges we may face and, to be honest, I do not want to know. I do not want my decisions to be influenced or affected by pre-sight. We have a mission to accomplish, one that affects everyone and we will succeed!"

With this final statement, Charlie sat back down to the applause of everyone in the room. He looked around him at the faces that were all turned in his direction. Charlie caught the eye of Jamie who even through his grief managed a slight smile of affirmation.

The alien, Dorak applauded with his arms out stretched in front of him and his long fingers slapping together, Commander Cunningham was standing clapping enthusiastically, and even Professor Davies seemed to break his sober persona even for a moment to congratulate his younger self on his motivational words. However, Charlie saw to his disappointment and confusion, a great sadness and strong suggestion of fear on Jason's face. Although his future son tried to mask his pain through the act of applause, Charlie could still make out a look of foreboding that seemed to be overwhelming the young man sitting across from him. Charlie showed no acknowledgement that he had seen this but the confidence he had shown moments before in his speech was tainted and doubt began to slip back into his thoughts.

# Chapter XXVIII

## *The Visitor*

After Charlie had sat down, a tray of drinks and food were delivered to the table and the team present helped themselves while they discussed the next part of the mission. As they talked, there was a sense of anticipation in the air. They were about to embark on the most important mission ever undertaken and everyone was on edge but restless to be off.

"I have signalled the *Blackbird* using our mobile homing beacon, and the ship has confirmed lock on to the signal," said Commander Cunningham re-entering the room after leaving some 15 minutes before. "The team are clearing an LZ and we have an ETA of 1 hour for the *Blackbird*."

"Good," acknowledged Professor Davies. "We will need to be leaving and heading south at first light tomorrow morning. Time, ironically, is running out and the bomb needs to be in place in exactly two days' time. Commander Cunningham, is everything prepared and will it be ready for departure?"

"Yes, Professor," the commander replied. Equipment, vehicles, supplies, are all packed in Loading Bay 3 of the *Blackbird* and ready to roll as soon as we are."

"Good," said the professor. "We should reach the Antarctic shelf by midday tomorrow, then set out with the caterpillars."

The professor smiled at Charlie's innocent confused face.

"Caterpillars," the professor repeated. "Off road transporters with caterpillar tracks to allow for driving on snow and ice. We cannot take the ship to the bomb release point because of its sheer weight. The concentration of volcanic vents in the vicinity provide extremely unstable and fragile ground that would be too weak to support the *Blackbird*. We will need to land the ship at edge of the of the ice flow where it is thickest and void of vents. From there we will strike out with caterpillars and hope that the cold does not freeze the engines otherwise, it is a long walk!"

"How long?" asked Charlie.

"Fifteen miles", interjected Jason. He had left his seat at the other side of the table and had come around to sit beside Charlie. "And, believe me," he continued. "You do not want to be around when that bomb goes off!" His face tried to crack a smile but it was obvious to Charlie that Jason was not feeling the positive vibes that the rest of the room seemed to be relishing in.

"What's wrong?" Charlie quietly asked.

Jason stared at Charlie for a moment as if he was just about to confess something incredible but all he replied was "Ask me again another time." And with that, Jason got up and quietly left the room.

Charlie began to stand up to follow but a gentle hand rested on his arm and beckoned him to sit back down. The professor slowly took his hand away and gave Charlie a kind sympathetic smile.

"We all have secrets to keep," he said. "We also have secrets to tell. Jason will choose whether to keep or tell in his own time. Be patient. Come, you have so many people to meet and I am sure many questions that need answered."

Professor Davies took Charlie over to Dorak who was deep in conversation with another alien.

"Dorak," the professor greeted him. Dorak looked up as the two men approached. "Dorak, this is my younger self, Charlie."

"An extreme pleasure to meet you," Dorak said in his metallic voice. "It has been a very long time coming but worth the wait." He extended a long-fingered hand toward Charlie who politely accepted it in a handshake. Dorak's hand felt cold, dry and leathery but the grip was firm and crushing. Charlie knew it was unintentional but Dorak's grip caused Charlie to subtly rub his sore hand after it was released.

"This is incredible," Charlie said. I have been amazed by everything I have seen up until now. I have stood on a holodeck, we have travelled through time, I've walked with dinosaurs, I have met myself as an old man, sorry, older man!" Charlie smiled as he saw the professors amused reaction to his latter comment. "I have glimpsed the future but I never thought I would meet an alien."

"We prefer the term 'other worlders', Dorak said. "To us, you are alien."

"Of course," Charlie said. "Sorry, I meant no offence."

"None taken," smiled Dorak. When my people first encountered yours, we reacted the same. We had never seen a sentient being that was unlike us."

"If you don't mind me asking, where are you from?" said Charlie.

"We are from a planet that exists just outside your own solar system," replied Dorak. "It is called *Tobold* and is one of forty planets orbiting around twin suns. It is very similar to your Earth. Our atmosphere is made up of the same elements as yours; nitrogen, oxygen, and argon which protect our planet from harmful ultraviolet solar radiation. Seventeen of the forty planets in our system orbit around *Mogor*, the larger of the two suns, while *Tobold* is one of the other twenty-three planets orbiting around the second star, *Gordot*. We do not have a moon as you do but tidal and gravitational shifts on our planet are dictated by the proximity of the other planets. The nearest one to *Tobold* is the equivalent distance from your earth to your moon, some 238857 miles.

"We have a similar respiratory system to humans and absorb air through two sets of lungs. Our planet is more water based than yours, almost 90% and we have developed towns and cities in the oceans and lakes to compensate for population expansion. We can survive without air 10 times longer than humans, allowing to dive to great depths.

"Our endoskeleton structure is stronger too with our bones containing a greater level of osseous tissue providing a higher tolerance to external pressure. This is particularly useful when diving deep and has helped us to adapt to our under-water lifestyle.

"We have been part of the EGU for 200 years ever since its team on Earth made contact with us at the edge of your solar system in the 26th century. The original dream and ambition of the EGU has now stretched across the stars with 429 planets taking similar action to discreetly help with their own environmental issues. Over the centuries, the letters of the organisation have stayed the same but the G now stands for "galactic". A secret intergalactic environmental task force, working together across space to protect the health of the universe."

*Lewis Davies*

Charlie felt the hairs on the back of his neck stand up. Was he really the founding father of this incredible organisation? It was hard to fathom that he would lead the galaxy towards a better future for all. Charlie began to feel scared. Again, he had the feeling that it was too much of a burden for him to carry. Surely someone else could plant the bomb? He didn't have to do it. As long as someone did, it didn't really matter who.

He was about to comment and confess his true feelings about the mission when an announcement came across the tannoy.

"The *Blackbird* will be arriving in 15 minutes. All ground crew please prepare for landing."

"Excellent," Professor Davies said. "We have bought you fresh supplies and power cells, Dorak. We have already begun clearing the *Avocet* of vegetation and you and your team should be able to take off within the next three hours."

"You know we cannot return to our own time until the mission is complete," Dorak said.

"I know," the professor acknowledged sadly. "Perhaps you would prefer a more hospitable location than this for the next two days?"

Dorak smiled. "The warm dark recesses of the Pacific Ocean may suit us better? I am afraid the harsh climate of the Antarctic would see my race dead before we had covered a mile."

"I understand," the professor nodded. "At least allow us to play host tonight, for dinner," he offered.

"It would be an honour, Professor," Dorak bowed and the professor mimicked.

The two friends then turned to Charlie. "Please excuse us," they both said. "We have affairs to attend to."

Charlie watched them leave and it dawned on him that he still had not had the opportunity to tell them he couldn't complete the mission and someone else would have to. He looked around for someone to talk to but everyone seemed preoccupied with someone else. Jamie was in deep conversation with one of the *Avocet's* team while commander Cunningham had gone to supervise the clearing of the landing zone for the *Blackbird*. Then it came to him. He would find Jason and discuss with him about the mission.    He had so many questions to ask. Perhaps that is what the professor referred to when he said Charlie had so many questions he wished answered?

Charlie slipped out of the room and into the maze of corridors that laced their way through the *Avocet*.

The ship was of similar design to the *Blackbird* but clearly a lot more advanced in terms of technology. Small automated carts rolled through the corridors, carrying variety of loads from medical supplies and vacuum-packed food to machinery parts and organic samples and materials. As Charlie explored, several figures shuffled passed him, going about their business. Charlie noticed their faces were devoid of life and it looked as if they were wearing masks. On closer inspection of one, he realised that they were not real people but robots. Charlie had seen something similar on television but that was someone pretending, dressed up to look like a robot. Cyborgs they were called. Cybernetic organisms. Machine on the inside but natural fibre and tissue on the outside to create an exoskeleton that looks like human.

Walking passed him was the real thing and as Charlie stared at it, without turning, it suddenly spoke. "Good day Professor Davies," it said in a familiar voice.

Charlie was confused, "Erm...hello!" he said. The robot carried on walking away down the corridor without any hesitation. Charlie blankly watched it disappear around a bend.

Suddenly, a loud laugh behind him made him jump and he spun around to see who was mocking him.

Leaning in the doorway of a room off to Charlie's left was Jason with a big grin on his face. "Good day Professor Davies," he said again smiling.

"It was you!" Charlie laughed holding his chest, feigning a heart attack. "I thought it was the bloody robot!"

"That was hilarious! The look on your face, come on" Jason beckoned Charlie into the room. "We have a lot to talk about."

∞

# Chapter XXIX

## *The Mistake*

"I should ground you," laughed Charlie as the two of them sat down in a room like the one that he and Jamie had been staying in.

"Not for another 10 years, Dad!" Jason teased, pouring them a drink.

The two of them sat without speaking for a couple of minutes when finally, it was Jason who spoke first.

"I know what you're thinking Dad," he said. "You can't stop it you know? Time has already dictated it will happen."

At this, Charlie jumped up, knocking over his glass of whisky and spilling its contents across the table.

"YES!" he shouted. "I know. My older self has already told me! I don't believe it! I don't care what you both say, I will not allow you to die and I do not believe that time cannot be changed! They have been doing it for fucking centuries!" Charlie waved his hands around directing his profanity to the rest of the ship.

"Dad," Jason calmly said. "I understand your frustration. You spoke like this so many times over the years but always, you accepted what will be will be! The changes that the EGU have made throughout time have already been written in history. My death in the raptor attack has already been written. Altering that will cause a shift in the time line and..."

"Jeopardising all existence, yes I know, I have heard it all before!!" Charlie interrupted. "But how can you just accept that? You know when you are going to die! That would drive me insane!"

"I have accepted my destiny as did Professor Young accept his," replied Jason, "Knowing when your time will come is not so bad. You can plan what life you have and when death comes, you are ready."

Charlie sat back down and Jason poured him another drink. In a quieter voice this time, he asked his son "and when will you be ready? When is your time?"

Jason leaned back in his chair, cradling his glass with both hands.

Clearly the question had had a deeper impact on him than Charlie thought as Jason's face became a mask of pain and tear began to well up in his eyes.

He hesitated for a moment as if trying to remember some pre-derived thought. "Four days ago," he softly whispered.

As if reading the confusion on Charlie's face, Jason continued.

"Four days ago, I was on a routine patrol with a reconnaissance team heading to the Cretaceous period with the intention of collecting some samples. We had found that some species of wetland plant could trap oxygen and store it. We were studying their qualities in an effort to create artificial gills to assist our Marine Division."

Charlie sat in silence listening to his son's story. The words were familiar to him having heard his older self tell the same tale only a day ago. Suddenly, Charlie realised that the words were a little too familiar, the same, in fact. It seemed as if Jason was reading a script, a script that Professor Davies had already read from. Trying not to feel suspicious, he brought his attention back to Jason.

"My father, that is.. you," Jason said "and Professor Young were also there. We were 10 minutes in to the mission and were navigating a large forest adjacent to a marsh where the plants grew when, velociraptors attacked us. They must have stalked us through the forest because they came at us from behind and knew exactly what they were doing. They took my father's leg and I did not survive."

There was a moment of reflection as this last piece of information sank in.

"How did you die?" Charlie gently asked.

"A velociraptor killed me." Jason said but there was no conviction in his voice. His answer was too vague for Charlie's curiosity but Charlie decided not to push it. Instead, he got up from the table and indicated to the toilet. Jason seemed to relax as if he had just been interrogated.

Once alone, Charlie had the chance to focus on the previous conversation. Jason was hiding something, that bit was true but what? From Jason's reaction and his older self's reaction to his questions, Charlie was aware that something tragic had occurred but felt that they were not being entirely truthful with him.

He would have to try to get them to open up but he did have time on his side so Charlie decided to wait until the mission was over before approaching them again on the matter.

He washed his hands and went to join Jason again. It wasn't every day you get to spend time with your future son and Charlie was going to make the most of it.

An announcement came over the tannoy, "The Blackbird has now landed. Could all immediate staff report to their posts? Lift off to Sector 7G tomorrow morning will be 07:00. Please would all teams be ready for boarding by 06:45? All Antarctic weather gear and equipment to be loaded by 05:45. Thank you."

"So," Charlie began. "What was your mother like?"

"What kind of a question is that?" Jason laughed.

"Well," Charlie replied, "I'm curious. Is she still alive, in your time, I mean?"

The atmosphere suddenly changed and darkness seemed to descend on the two.

"She died when I was very young," Jason said sadly. "My father told me she was a geneticist and specialised in hereditary diseases. She came into contact with an unknown virus on a moon orbiting Jupiter. She was dead before they got her back to earth. It rapidly attacked her nervous system shutting down her heart. My father never got to say goodbye."

"What do you remember of her?" Charlie asked softly.

"Not much," said Jason. "Images really. She had a kind face and was very beautiful. I remember blond hair and gentle blue eyes. My father told me her name was Hannah and they had known each other since school. He still misses her deeply and it has been 70 years. Longevity of life may not always be a good thing!"

"Could you have not travelled back to prevent it happening?" Charlie asked. Again, his thoughts stemmed to saving Jason.

"Death cannot be controlled, it cannot be avoided!" Jason stammered. "Don't you get it yet? We have all this technology now. We can travel through time, shape the future, save worlds but we cannot stop someone dying! The repercussions would be devastating. They got it wrong at the beginning. Nobody really understood the limitations of time travel. We felt we could change anything until one of the early scientists involved with developing time travel tried to save his teenage daughter from a car accident.

He travelled back and warned her, she decided not to take her car out on that particular day. The knock-on effect was a ripple in the time line causing nineteen people to die in a follow up crash caused by the very same truck the scientist's daughter would have encountered. Coincidence perhaps? No. It was proven to be of a direct result of the truck not interacting with the car the scientist's daughter would have been driving."

"But he saved his daughter!" Charlie said.

"Not in the long term and at what cost?" Jason asked. The daughter could not live with the guilt of 19 people dying because of her actions and she committed suicide two days after the crash. The scientist could not have foreseen this as it did not show up on the time line until he intervened. So, all he would have known before travelling back was that his daughter had died in a car crash."

"What happened to the scientist?" Charlie asked.

"He came back to his work but swore he would never intervene with death again. His vow became part of the constitution regarding time travel and restrictions were placed on all travel in to the past. Only people who were part of the programme were cleared to travel backwards through time and a *Restriction to Travel Act* was passed which we all had to sign. So, do you see? You cannot save someone from death. Professor Young knew that better than anyone!"

"Professor Young?" Charlie gasped. "He was the scientist?"

"Yes" said Jason. "It was his daughter Lucy who should have died in the crash. Instead, it caused a butterfly effect that ended more than one life that day and inevitably didn't save hers."

"A butterfly effect?" asked Charlie, a little confused.

"A butterfly effect" answered Jason, "is when a small action causes a larger reaction. It is said if a butterfly flaps its wings in America, it could cause a tidal wave in Japan. You could perhaps refer to the phenomenon as a snowball gaining size and momentum as it rolls down the hill; small at first but getting larger. Every action we will ever take will have its consequences and some of those consequences will affect us all."

The two men sat for a moment sipping their drinks. It was Jason again who spoke first.

"I know it is hard to accept," he said, "that you may not be able to save me from death but the decisions you make will define the future and you must not deviate from the plan set before you." Jason reached up behind his head and unclipped a silver chain that was around his neck. He gently pulled the rest of the chain from out the front of his tunic and Charlie could finally see a small amulet hanging from it. Jason offered the chain to Charlie.

"I was told to give this to you when I felt the time was right." Jason said. "It was given to me by Dorak, 30 years ago. He spoke of a time that decisions will need to be made that will change the course of all."

Charlie nervously took the amulet and turned it over in his hand. It felt warm and not just because it had been resting in Jason's tunic but it seemed to have an inner heat emanating from its core. Now Charlie was actually holding it in his hand and not seeing it in a photo, he could see it was the size of a £2-pound coin but weighed almost nothing. It was made of stone, shaped like a butterfly flapping its wings and the strange markings etched into its surface gave off a faint blue glow.

"I have seen this before," he said, "in a book."

"It is made from the rock of Tobold, Dorak's home planet and has a chemical quality that reacts with heat giving off an azure blue light. The Tobold's believe the mineral inside the stone has a healing quality that they have used for millennia to prolong life. It was their studies into this quality that assisted us in developing our own techniques and science in ageing.

"When Dorak told me to give you the amulet when I felt the time was right, I had no idea when that time would be. We are on the eve of the most important chapter in the history of the universe, we must not fail and knowing what I know will come to pass, I now know the time has come that we need all the help we can get and whether the amulet has healing properties or not, it can't hurt to believe, can it?"

Jason ended the last sentence with a forced joviality that Charlie noticed instantly and again he felt suspicious of Jason and his sincerity. "Know what I know," he said. What does he know? Charlie's head was a whirl of questions, thoughts and suspicions. His next question was on the tip of his tongue when an announcement came over the tannoy.

∞

# Chapter XXX

## *The Departure*

"Would all relevant personnel please prepare to switch aircraft? Departure time for the *Phoenix* will be in 30 minutes."

Charlie placed the amulet around his neck and followed Jason out of the room and down the corridors back to the entrance hatch to the *Phoenix*. Jamie and the rest of the expedition had already assembled and preparations were made for the trip to the Antarctic.

Additional supplies from both ships were being transferred across as Charlie once again, took in the sheer size of the *Blackbird* now dwarfing the much smaller *Phoenix*. Charlie could now see the *Phoenix* in its entirety after the ground crews had cleared it of vegetation earlier. It was sleeker than the *Blackbird* with a reflective chrome surface. A faint blue glow seemed to crawl underneath the ship's hull making it strangely difficult to make out a definite shape as if it was a mirage shifting in the desert or the shimmer above a hot road.

Professor Davies was talking quietly with Dorak at the entrance ramp to the *Blackbird* while a number of Tobold's were shaking hands or embracing members of the *Blackbird's* team.

Charlie saw Jamie helping with some boxes and went over to see him.

"How you getting on?" Charlie asked slapping his friend on the back.

"I'm better," Jamie replied quietly but it was obvious to Charlie that his friend was still mourning for the loss of Professor Young.

"What you been up to?"

"I spent a little time on the *Phoenix's* holodeck," Jamie answered. "Did a bit of re-enactment from *Scarface*. You know the bit where he has the machine gun and just let's rip? Yeah, well, it felt good!"

Charlie smiled at his friend. "Say hello to my little friend!" was Jamie's favourite movie line and used it regularly when discussing the complexities of dating and what he would say to any girl he was lucky enough to attract the interest of. It was always a sexual reference to him dropping his trousers.

Charlie laughed. I can just imagine you being in that film. You would make a great Al Pacino!"

Jamie smiled back and gave his friend a long hug. "Thanks mate," he said quietly. "I appreciate that."

One of the soldiers from the *Blackbird* was passing through the ensemble with a camera taking pictures of his friends and colleagues. Creating the memories that all would look back on and remember with great fondness of a more peaceful time.

"Why don't we get a photo taken, show off that new scar of yours?" suggested Jamie indicating to Charlie's cheek which was still red and raw from the pygmy attack. The two boys smiled and went over to the photographer.

They stood next to each other, arms round each other's shoulders. Several other members gathered round behind them as the photographer lined up his lens. At the last second, Charlie decided to reach into his tunic and pulled out the chain with the amulet hanging from it, leaving it lying outside his top. The camera shutter clicked and the cameraman passed the instant photo to Charlie.

"That explains it," Jamie smiled, as they looked upon the same picture they saw in the photo album back on the *Blackbird*. "If the photos are anything to go by then next stop, Antarctica and the exploding Thermos!"

Charlie laughed. "If only that was all it was, a Thermos then I wouldn't be so paranoid that it was all going to blow up in our faces!"

"You know what everyone is saying," replied Jamie. "We have to succeed. We *do* succeed; otherwise none of this will exist!"

"I know mate, I know but I can't help feeling that we are not being told everything. There is something not quite right about it all and I am worried that it will not be as straight forward as they are making it out to be."

"Come on bud." Jamie put his arm around Charlie shoulder and turned him toward the *Blackbird*. It will be fine. I am here, you are here, Professor Davies is here and your son is here. With a team like that, we can't be beat!"

Charlie saw the smile on his friends face drop. "I am truly sorry, Jamie," he said sadly. If it is any consolation, you contribute to so much in your long life. Your future is an incredible journey and you should be proud of all you have achieved, all you will achieve and I will be with you every step of the way."

Jamie wiped a tear from his eye. "What will be will be, right?" he sniffed. Let's just make sure he didn't die for nothing! I don't want any more doubt or uncertainty. We are going to plant this bomb and save the universe! Ok?"

"Ok Jamie." Charlie kindly smiled as he took his friends hand in shake.

They turned and took one last look at Dorak and his team, standing at the foot of the entrance hatch to the *Phoenix*. Charlie and Jamie simultaneously bowed and the crew of the *Phoenix* returned the honour. With one final look, the boys turned and headed up the entrance ramp of the *Blackbird*.

∞

Once on the observation deck, Charlie and Jamie joined Professor Davies, Jason and Commander Cunningham at the viewing window.

The *Phoenix* was preparing for take-off and its vertical thrusters had already rotated around to give it maximum lift out of the forest clearing. As the *Blackbird* watched, the ship in front of it fired up its engines and began to slowly climb up into the night air. On the *Blackbird*, there was a feeling of sadness and abandonment as the *Phoenix* finally disappeared over the tops of the trees.

After a moments silence, Professor Davies turned to the rest of those present. "Gentlemen," he said, "we are on the eve of a great adventure. One that will change the fate of all. We leave tomorrow at 7:00 hours so I suggest that we all get some rest."

Commander Cunningham concurred and added "Please be ready for briefing at 06:00."

With that, the team dispersed and headed their separate ways. Charlie and Jamie went to their room, had a meal in almost silence only making light conversation about the quality of the food. After their showers, both boys retired to bed, haunted by their own thoughts of what was to come.

As Charlie drifted off to sleep, he still could not shake the foreboding feeling that Professor Davies and Jason were keeping something from him and that the next two days held more than just an incredible mission to save the universe. Something more terrifying was to come.

∞

# Chapter XXXI

## *The 2nd Departure*

He was screaming "grab the rope, just hold on! Don't do it!" but the rope went slack, the crevasse fell silent and he knew that there was no hope left. After all they had been through, it seemed all for nothing now he was gone, lost in the darkness.

Charlie was left hanging, spinning gently. His gloved hand still held onto the other end of the rope while the rest trailed down into the darkness below. A familiar voice above him screamed "come on, pull him up, we've got to go!" as he felt a wild tug and was forcibly dragged up the precipice wall.

Charlie woke with a start to find himself in his dark room on board the *Blackbird*. He spent the rest of the night drifting in and out of a disturbed sleep full of mixed visions containing images of Jason, Professor Davies, Jamie and dark, never-ending tunnels. Screams could be heard coming from the tunnels and always was the presence of the amulet; glowing blue and beautifully terrifying.

∞

The next morning, Charlie did not feel he could share his dreams with Jamie, so they shared a breakfast, got dressed into their polar survival gear and headed to the observation deck for Professor Cunningham's briefing.

When they arrived, everyone was already assembled and Professor Cunningham had already called up the holographic display depicting the tunnel where the bomb was to be deposited.

"Due to the tear in the timeline, our records of the previous missions to plant the explosive are becoming more and more clouded. As the rip expands, even our own memory of accounts is shifting like a dream that we can't quite remember. Although previous loops have been successful, the rip has thinned the time line making our success more uncertain. This could be the last loop and chance to repair the crack. Although for many of us, this has already been part of our past, if we don't do whatever it takes and succeed again this time, there will be no past or future for any of us."

There was a murmur of concern around the room and Charlie realised this was the first time that he had sensed real doubt in the group. A hand grabbed his shoulder.

Professor Davies stood in front of him.

"Are you ready?" he asked.

"You should know," smiled Charlie.

"Since every loop has caused the rip in the timeline to grow, my memories of this moment are becoming vaguer," said the professor. "A lot of time has passed for me since this moment but I still recall the feeling of determination and excitement of the time. I feel it now."

"Yes," agreed Charlie. I am terrified but eager to begin. The adrenaline is pumping through me. I cannot wait to lift off."

"You won't have much longer to wait," interrupted Commander Cunningham. "The countdown will begin in 5 minutes." He then walked over to the observation screen and spoke into a microphone. "5 minutes until departure. Make sure all cargo bay doors are locked securely, the outer perimeter is clear of debris and fauna."

"Co-ordinates are set, Sir." Spoke one of Cunningham's operators sitting at a panel and button covered console. "4 minutes until lift off, making our arrival time at Antarctic Point 0210 in one hour. All Extreme Terrain vehicles and personnel are standing by."

"Thank you, Lieutenant," said the Commander. He walked back and joined Professor Davies, Charlie and Jamie at the round briefing table in the centre of the room.

Everyone was quiet, not making eye contact and the silence was only broken when the countdown began for departure.

Even when the engines roared into life and the ship ascended into the South American morning sky, no one spoke; the only movement the made was to strap themselves into their seats.

Below the ship, the jungle slowly came back to life and as the *Blackbird* disappeared in a flash, a young family of tapir entered the clearing unaware of the significance of what came before carrying the future of all with it.

∞

# Chapter XXXII

## *The Ice*

Through the observation window, Charlie could see the white expanse of the Antarctic stretching beyond the horizon. The vast bleakness of the snow and ice was a startling contrast to the lush green carpet of the South American rainforest.

It had been one hour since they had taken off from the clearing in the jungle. Charlie had sat and watched the now familiar changes outside the obs window but hardly noticed as they approached the Antarctic LZ. Hardly a word had been spoken except for a few light-hearted exchanges.

For the second time in an hour the monotony was broken by a voice over the tannoy.

"We are approaching the LZ, please prepare for final descent."

Those that had got out of their seats after lift-off returned to their positions around the table, while the rest strapped themselves in.

"This is it!" Jamie said to Charlie with a nervous grin.

The two friends felt the shudder of the *Blackbird* touching down on the polar ice pack and the reverse engines sent up clouds of snow that could be seen on the many monitors around the room.

The tannoy came back to life. "All engines convert to standby, ground crew prepare frost reduction on all external landing gear. Control to Bridge; Commander, loading bay 1 is readying your ground support. Please be ready for departure in 15 minutes. We have reports of a severe weather front coming in from the west. It will intercept your course in 30 minutes."

Professor Davies stood up and addressed the room.

"My friends, we stand on the brink of the most important moment in history. Without it there will be no future. We must not fail. As you all know, although history dictates that we will succeed, recent strains on the timeline have disrupted moments that have come before to the point that any deviation from the true path could spell failure." The professor let this sink in for a moment then continued.

"The report of a storm coming in is a prime example that nothing is certain. We have not encountered a storm at this stage in the mission but we must endure and go through it. We cannot wait for it to pass, we must carry on. We must succeed! Please prepare yourselves, we depart in 10 minutes."

With those powerful and frightening words echoing around his head, Charlie followed the rest of the team out of the observation room into the turbo-lift that would take them down to the loading bays.

As soon as the doors closed, Jamie leaned over to Charlie and whispered "have you spoken to Jason yet?"

Charlie put his finger to his lips. "No, I haven't" he whispered back. "I will when the time is right. We need to plant this bomb, and then I will speak to him. Ironically, I have time on my hands."

Their private conversation was interrupted by a sudden blast of freezing wind striking them directly in the face.

"Wrap up people" shouted Commander Cunningham over the howling wind now swirling round the loading bay.

Crew members were hurrying around, struggling to secure the equipment into their sled. A few the ground crew were preparing the All-Terrain Vehicles for the extremely low temperatures they were about to face. Hoses snaked their way across the loading bay floor as they supplied hot anti-freeze steam to the mechanisms and gears of the vehicles.

Charlie and Jamie stepped into the rear ATV and strapped themselves into the back-seat. Professor Davies and Jason joined them with Jason taken a seat in the front. Commander Cunningham entered the front ATV. Charlie's vehicle door slid shut and jolted forward, the tank like caterpillar tracks driving them out into the icy wilderness beyond.

As the ATV's pulled away from the *Blackbird* and the ships loading doors closed behind them, Charlie couldn't shake the ominous feeling that there was something that Professor Davies and Jason were still not telling the whole truth about the mission. What awaited them in the frozen wastes of the Antarctic? Again, he doubted was it so simple that they would drive out to the middle of the ice, plant a bomb and save the universe?

Only time would tell!

# Chapter XXXIII

## *The Separation*

They had been travelling for 20 minutes and the *Blackbird* was now nothing more than a dark shadow in the distance. Charlie reckoned they were driving at a steady pace of 60 miles an hour and the weather was being kind to them. The ice underneath them was solid and a fresh dusting of snow just before they left the ship, gave the landscape a crisp glittering texture.

The conversation within the vehicles was a light hearted one with Professor Davies, Jason and Charlie sharing stories of Charlie's childhood and how similar Jason was at the same age.

Jamie had fallen asleep with his head leaning against the dark window when suddenly he was violently jolted awake by the ATV shuddering over on to its left side.

The passengers all started screaming at once while the ATV in front ground to a halt and the front team piled out and came running back to assist.

"Everybody out, move, move, move" screamed Jason.

Jamie quickly came to and looked over to Charlie. His friend had already swung his own door open and was grabbing the hand of one of the mission team from the front ATV. Jamie felt another jolt and the window next to him caved in covering him in glass.

"Get out of there Jamie," begged Charlie offering the end of a ski pole.

"I can't!" Jamie panicked, looking down at the foot well. "My leg is trapped."

The ATV gave another shudder and Jamie screamed out with pain. As he turned back to Charlie, it could be clearly seen that the left side of his face was covered in blood. A large shard of glass was embedded just above his left eye. "Help me", he cried.

"I'm trying!" panicked Charlie. "Try and grab the pole."

Though partially blinded, Jamie reached down and managed to grab the top of his boot. With a strength he never knew he had, Jamie pulled at his leg as hard as he could. A searing pain shot through it and with a sound like a branch snapping, his leg finally came free. Jamie again, screamed with pain but although he felt close to passing out, managed to grab the end of the ski pole and Charlie pulled him out.

Immediately Jamie was dragged away from the wrecked ATV and the team medic began to treat him. Jamie was screaming in pain and apart from the piece of glass embedded in his eye, Jamie had also suffered from a severe broken leg. Charlie could see the shin bone sticking out through the skin.

"Just breath," the medic advised him. "I'm going to give you some morphine to help with the pain."

Jamie's screams and writhing became less as the medic stabilised and applied a splint to Jamie's leg while the glass in his eye was taped securely, the area cleaned and covered.

"I cannot remove it here," the medic stated. "The point of the shard is too close to the optic nerve. Removing it without the proper medical equipment stored in the *Blackbird* could cause severe infection. At the very least, he will lose his eye but we can only hope that is all. I only brought the essential medical supplies for our journey. He has to get back to the ship."

The moment was interrupted by a loud grinding sound and for the first time, Charlie noticed the carnage around him. The surrounding snow was stained red with Jamie's blood and the ATV they had been in moments before, was tilted at a 70° angle in a large fissure that had opened in the ice. Some of the team were frantically trying to salvage equipment from the back of the ATV but were interrupted by the vehicle sliding slowly into the crack. Jamie's injuries had been sustained from his side of the vehicle being crushed by the wall of the crack and as the team watched, the ATV slipped over onto its side and sunk into the ice.

Commander Cunningham was the first to speak.

"We will have to continue on foot. The ice is too thin for vehicles. Smith, take the remaining ATV and Jamie back to the *Blackbird*. Take squad two with you. We have lost a lot of the food supplies down that hole and we now don't have enough for everyone. Professor Davies, Jason, myself, Charlie, and squads one and three will continue. Pack the sleds; we need to leave in five minutes. Fortunately, the bomb was in the first ATV. Load it on the sled. Stay in radio contact for as long as you can and watch out for that storm warning. It may pass us by but this accident had not occurred during any of our previous missions. We cannot predict anything now. Good luck gentlemen."

Charlie helped members of squad two lift Jamie onto a stretcher and slide it into the back of the remaining ATV. "Take care mate," he whispered with tears in his eyes. "I'll see you when I get back." Jamie showed no signs of hearing his friend and Charlie's hand gently slipped from Jamie's as the door was closed.

"Come on Charlie," Jason said gently putting his arm around the boy's shoulders. "We have to go."

Charlie turned away from the ATV and took the set of ski poles offered to him by one of the team continuing. The rest of the squads had already set off, while the ATV's engine roared back into life and turned towards the *Blackbird*. Charlie quickly wiped away the rapidly freezing tears on his cheeks, gave the ATV and his friend inside, one last glance and turned towards his destiny.

# Chapter XXXIV

## *The Fall*

The trek was slow and hard going. Only five miles in, the team found themselves faced with another large fissure crossing their path. A makeshift bridge had to be made at the expense of one of the sleds leading to an increase in what everyone had to carry. Charlie's pack now contained the bomb, along with 60ft of rope, some food supplies, and the radio. Many items had to be abandoned and it looked increasingly like it was going to be a one-way trip.

"How are you bearing up?" the Professor asked, joining Charlie towards the back of the pack.

"I'm ok," Charlie answered. I'm just thinking. How are we going to get back from this, even if we do make it to the drop point? But surely, we must, otherwise you and Jason wouldn't be here. None of this would be happening."

"Unfortunately, it is not as simple as that anymore," the professor answered. "You know everything is now hanging in the balance. Even I do not know what the future holds any more. All I know now is that we must plant that bomb. Whatever happens after that is for the future to decide."

Charlie began to feel his face go numb and pulled his protective visor further over his nose.

"Frostbite can set in quickly" The professor said. "Make sure you don't have any skin exposed to the air."

A whirring, crackling sound emanated from Charlie's pack.

"Commander Cunningham," a metallic voice said. "Do you copy? Come in Commander, this is the *Blackbird*. Do you read?"

The commander reached in to Charlie's pack and pulled out the radio receiver. "Commander here. Report. What is it Jones?"

"Sir," the radio voice replied. "We've been monitoring that storm we picked up earlier. It's coming at you fast! You better batten down and wait for it to blow over."

"No can do, Jones," the commander shouted above the sudden buildup of wind. "We've got to push on. The bomb must be placed at the exact time. We have to go on. We're two miles out from the vent. We can't stop now. Gentlemen, join up your life lines. Make sure you are tightly connected to the man in front. I'll take point. Jason take rear."

The wind was now stirring up the snow, causing visibility to drop to 10%. "SET YOUR GPS TO .30 ON A HEADING OF 78°", the commander screamed above the roaring storm now raging around them. "STAY ON COURSE".

The team pushed on through the storm. Charlie could not see the man in front that he was tied to, nor could he see his own feet. It took all his strength to stay up. He was being battered from all sides by the wind and he felt like he was being pebble dashed as freezing sleet tore at his clothes.

They stumbled on blindly what seemed like an hour but it had only been 10 minutes. Charlie began to lose feeling in his feet and he feared he may pass out from exhaustion. From time to time, the team had to wade through thick snow drifts. Adding to the unsure footing on the slippery ice, Charlie's strength was rapidly waning and it was only the tightening of the rope in front and the gentle tug if he started to lag, that kept him upright.

Suddenly he heard a scream behind him, was pulled off his feet and was dragged along the ice backwards. He tried to grab hold of something to slow himself down but the ice was too smooth and he found no rough edges to catch.

Without warning, the ground beneath him suddenly disappeared and Charlie felt himself falling into dark, emptiness but he quickly came to a sharp, abrupt halt. He screamed in pain as the rope tied around him went taut and he felt two of his ribs break. The rushing wind, ice and snow immediately stopped as if someone had flipped a switch and as Charlie's eyes grew accustomed to the dark, he could make out the smooth, flawless wall of a crevasse.

In the gloom 20 meters below him, Charlie could just see a figure hanging on the end of the rope he was tied to. The figure was not struggling but hanging limp with its body arched at the waist where the rope was tied.      Its legs hung loosely and as the body rotated and the figures hood had fallen back as its head hung, Charlie finally made out the face of the person below him. It was Jason! His face was bloodied and there was a deep gash on the left side of his head. His eyes were closed     and     he     was     completely unresponsive to Charlie's calls.

Charlie felt another jolt as he suddenly dropped 10 more meters and came to a sharp halt. Jason still hung motionless below him.

"Jason!!" Charlie screamed, but Jason did not move. Frantic shouts above were now echoing down to the two hanging men.

"Charlie, Jason! You two ok?"

"A couple of broken ribs I think but I'm fine," Charlie shouted back, "but Jason isn't! He's hurt his head and not responding! I don't know if he's dead or unconscious!"

"We're going to get you out of there. Just hang on!"

"Don't have much choice," Charlie shouted back angrily. Panic was beginning to set in as he stared at Jason's lifeless body. Not knowing if his son was alive or dead, Charlie became oblivious of his own danger and could only think of getting to Jason.

"Will you hurry the fuck up and get us out of here?" he screamed.

The commander called back. "We're trying but the rope is snagged. We can't seem to pull you up. Can see you see where its caught?"

Charlie looked up and could see that the rope had looped around a large piece of ice jutting out of the chasm wall. From the light above, he could also see the rope being pulled; going taut then loose has the team above tried to rescue them. As he watched, Charlie noticed that with every pull, the rope was beginning to fray as it rubbed against the razor-sharp ice which held it.

"Stop!!" he screamed. "The rope is snapping!"

"You're going to have to pull yourself up and unhook it. We can't get it from here."

"Are you fucking kidding??" Charlie was beginning to think he and Jason would never get out. "I can't pull Jason up with me. You're going to have to send another rope down."

"We don't have any more rope," the commander called back. You *have* to climb up! I'm sorry but we have no other choice!"

Charlie knew in his heart it was hopeless. He couldn't possibly haul the limp body of Jason up with him but he had to get out of the precipice. He still had the bomb strapped to his back and knew it was imperative that he got it back up to the surface.

Again, he felt a jolt as a snapping sound came from above and several strands of rope were cut by the ice.

"We're running out of time!" called the commander. "Charlie, you have to cut Jason loose. It's your only chance!"

"Nnnnnooooo!!!"" Charlie's scream echoed around the chasm. "Fuck you! I can't do that. I don't even know if he's alive but I'm not leaving him."

"There's no other way, Charlie. I'm sorry but everything will cease to be unless you plant that bomb. You know what's at stake. I'm so sorry but you have to cut him loose and climb up!"

Charlie's head was spinning. His eyes welled up with tears as the realisation of his situation dawned on him. He had no choice.

"I can't do it!" he cried, looking down. "I can't sacrifice my son."

"You won't have to," said Jason staring back up at him. He had been unconscious from the blow to the head caused by a falling piece of ice but had come to and was holding his hunting knife against the rope linking him to Charlie.

"Wh..what are you doing?" stammered Charlie.

"Saving us all," replied Jason. "I always knew this was how it would end for me. I just couldn't tell you because you wouldn't have agreed to come. You need to follow the plan, Charlie. Only you can bring stability to the universe."

"You told me you were killed by a raptor!" Charlie sobbed. "You lied!"

"Of course I lied," Jason replied. "Professor Davies had told me that you would try to save me if you knew the details of my death, so I *had* to lie! I'm so sorry Charlie, but this is the only way."

The rope above snapped some more against its holding and the two of them dropped a few meters more in to the precipice.

Charlie was fully crying now as he stared down at Jason.

"The rope won't hold both of us. You have to complete the mission, Charlie. You must climb out of here now and go on without me. Please, be strong. This is not the end for us, it is just the beginning. I love you Dad. See you in the future." Jason never took his eyes off Charlie and with one last smile of acceptance, cut through the rope that linked them together.

"Jason!!!!" Charlie screamed as his son fell and disappeared into the darkness below.

# Chapter XXXV

## *The Lie*

"Jason!!" Charlie screamed again but it was fruitless. Jason was gone and Charlie knew it.

He felt another jolt and several more strands of the rope gave way.

"Get out of there, NOW!!!" came the commanders voice.

With tears still welling up in his eyes, Charlie began to pull himself up the rope. His broken ribs were causing him excruciating pain and his head was becoming dizzy from the effort. He continued to pull himself up the rope using a strength he did not know he had. When he got to the overhang where the rope was snagged, he could see that it had almost been cut through. As he pulled himself carefully over the jutting piece of ice, the lower part of the rope finally gave and Charlie screamed as he began to fall. Luckily, what had tragically been Jason's doom was now Charlie's saviour as the front of one of the straps on his rucksack caught the overhang, causing him to crash into the jutting ice. He screamed again in pain as his damaged ribs hit hard against the wall. Now the tension had been taken away from the rope, the rest of it attached to the trooper out on the ice now hung within Charlie's grasp and he quickly grabbed it with both hands.

"Pull me up!!" he yelled.

He felt a jolt and almost lost his grip as the rope was tugged upwards with him hanging from it. Just when he though he couldn't hold on any longer, he lifted his head up and could see hands reaching down to him, grabbing his jacket, the straps of his ruck sack, and with one final pull, Charlie landed back out on the ice.

∞

Immediately he stood up and stumbled towards his older self who was standing watching with sadness on his face.

*Lewis Davies*

"YOU KNEW!" Charlie bellowed as he swung a left fist at the professor, hitting him across the face and knocking him to the ground. "You knew Jason was going to die there and you did NOTHING!"

"We did know." The professor replied rubbing his jaw, "but we didn't know when. If I could have stopped it, I would have but I'm sorry. We could not pinpoint exactly when it would happen so could not avoid it. Jason is gone but the mission isn't. We have to move on!"

Charlie was enraged. Two of the team, were holding his arms, preventing him from lashing out again.

"I HATE YOU!"

∞

The rest of the team were re-gathering equipment together and preparing to set off again.

Commander Cunningham approached Charlie and gently put his arm around his shoulder. "Come on," he said in a quiet voice. "We better move."


For the next hour, the team pushed on in silence. Professor Davies led while Charlie dragged his feet at the back of the line.

The wind was beginning to subside and visibility was improving. Out of the fading storm, the team could finally make out a range of sharp, jutting mountains which now loomed high above them. Word filtered along the line that their destination was ahead and, without further incident, the ETA should be 15 minutes.

As the they entered a canyon that led through the mountains, the sun began to set behind them, casting shadows across the sparkling powder white snow.

Charlie was last to enter the rocky terrain that the team had now halted in. Commander Cunningham and the professor were scrutinising a folded-out map while a few of the other men had their GPS transmitters out and were attempting to pick up a signal.

"According to map and the GPS readings, the ventilation shaft should be just behind that ridge," said the professor, pointing west. "The temporal shift in the timeline is distorting our signals but I vaguely remember those three peaks and that looks like a trail through to the vent. Go get Charlie."

"I'm here." Charlie said with noticeable disdain in his voice. He approached the two men mulling over the map. "Let's get this over and done with." He walked past the professor without even making eye contact and headed in the direction of an obvious track leading further in between the mountains.

The professor turned to the commander. "I just wish I could have told him the truth," he whispered sadly, and with a deep sigh, turned to follow Charlie and the rest of the team into the canyon.

∞

# Chapter XXXVI

## *The Choice*

After 10 minutes of hiking across loose scree and traversing around large boulders they finally arrived at the prehistoric volcanic vent where the bomb was to be placed.

The entrance was a gaping hole in the ground, 10 meters across and there was pale steam emanating from it. The snow and ice around the hole had melted and there was a noticeable warmth to the air in the direct vicinity of the vent.

Immediately the team started preparing for Charlie to slide down the vent by securing a life line around a pillar of solid rock some 30 meters away from the vent entrance. Mooring pegs were hammered in to the ground at intervals while the rope was secured at each peg until the remainder of the rope was curled at the entrance to the hole.

"Ok, Charlie," said the Professor helping him off with the rucksack containing the bomb. "We need at least 45 minutes to get to the safe zone once the bomb has been triggered and it will take 5 minutes to pull you back up the vent so you will only have 5 minutes down there to plant the bomb and set it. Do you understand?"

Charlie did not respond. He was still mad at his older self and it took all his self-restrain not to hit the old man again.

"I said, do you understand?" asked the professor again.

"I heard you!" shouted Charlie.

As the life line was attached to Charlie's safety harness, the professor continued to address his younger self but now with a voice that sounded like he had been here before. A voice of compassion, a voice of empathy.

"Charlie. I know you are mad at me for not telling you about Jason but if I had, would you have come? Would you believe me if I again said that all of this, Professor Young's death, Jamie's accident, and Jason falling, *must* happen for the future to be saved? Charlie, I know you will find this hard to accept, but things *are* happening for a reason and in order. It will be so very difficult for you to accept at this time. Believe me, I know. I still vividly remember how heartbroken I was, how heartbroken you are now to have had to watch Jason fall, disappearing into the black abyss. That image has never left me and it still haunts my dreams."

The professor's eyes were watering heavily and not because of any wind or cold. The air in the canyon was still and the heat from the vent hid the clouds of breath associated with cold climates.

Professor Davies was visibly crying as the overwhelming emotions took hold.

"I remember afterwards hating myself for allowing these things to happen. For not saving the ones I love. I also remember though, no matter what I tried to do to prevent things, this moment and everything that came before it was already set and I couldn't change that. As much as I was grieving, I had an incredibly strong sense of direction and determination to make things right and complete the mission. Nothing will get in your way to achieving this goal. It has happened so many times before and must happen again."

The professor took out a handkerchief and wiped his eyes.

Charlie looked up at the professor for the first time and there was a re-found look of strength and hope in his eyes. For the first time since his outburst, Charlie spoke.

"You told me that each loop in the timeline was making the rip worse, right?"

"Yes," agreed the professor. "every time we have to replay this mission, the rip is increasing making it more difficult to predict each outcome. Hence, why we could not calculate exactly where the Avocet would be or when..." the professor bowed his head. "or when Jason would fall."

Charlie began to become more animated.

"Well," he said. What if we didn't follow your past. What if we didn't complete the mission this time? The rip in the timeline could tear exponentially perhaps resetting itself?"

The professor looked up at Charlie, mouth open.

"It won't work," he said. "It's all already happened and that determines the future."

"One possible future," replied Charlie. "there are infinite possibilities, infinite timelines that could be created from even one simple action. Perhaps there are multiverses where our timelines are not controlled by destiny, by a preordained set of rules. Yes, there will be similarities between timelines, but the butterfly effect dictates that even the change in one molecule could alter the outcome."

"I don't know!! The rip in the timeline is distorting everything," panicked the professor, shaking his head. "I don't remember any of this!" He was visibly nervous and a look of confusion spread across his face.

"That's what I'm talking about," said Charlie excitedly. "If you don't remember this moment, then we are changing your past, and if we are changing your past and not following the predestined route, then why are we still here? Surely, everything should cease to be the moment we divert from the mission?"

One of the team politely interrupted. "Sir, we need to lower Charlie down the vent now! It's almost zero hour and we need to get the bomb in position and clear back to the safe zone."

The professor wasn't listening. He was staring at Charlie and sighed.

"You are right, Charlie. You are absolutely right! With every action, there has to be a reaction." He stammered as if reawakening and seeing everything clearly for the first time. "According to my history, if you don't plan the bomb, then the future cannot exist but it must exist otherwise we would not be here. The rip must be shifting this part of the timeline and creating a new one!

"That is the only explanation I can think of. The timeline is ripped in half. This half includes everything up until now, including my possible future, but the other half has not yet been written. Imagine a piece of string snapping and then reattaching the first piece to a different piece of string. You create a new ending to the piece of string.

"No matter what happens in your future, you will be the one to decide, not destiny. You make your own timeline. I finally understand! None of this should have happened. We did what we were told to do, what we were led to believe was set in stone. We followed others beliefs, what had come before when we should have followed the faith we have in ourselves. Our decisions are not for others to make. We need to undo all of this, reverse what has been done. Our decisions will build our future."

Charlie smiled. "You're a wise man Professor Davies."

"I take after you," the professor laughed.

Suddenly there was a deafening crack of thunder above them and blindingly in the dying light of dusk, a startling white light from above illuminated the people on the ground and the surrounding mountains.

Everyone looked up to see a bright tear in the dark, star speckled sky that seemed to ripple and move like expanding rings on the surface of water after a stone had been dropped in.

The tear was expanding revealing more blinding white light and the edges of the tear pulsated with multiple luminescent colours similar to the Aurora Australis. A wind was rising and started to whip at the teams clothing making it difficult to stand still.

"It's the rip in the timeline!" Professor Davies shouted above the increasingly deafening wind. "It's going to tear this reality apart. We need to get back to the Blackbird and try and jump forward to the 24th Century! The increasing distortion in time may give us a window of opportunity and enough force to slingshot us in to the remaining timeline."

"It's too late," shouted Charlie. "Look!"

The tear had grown and there was now a swirling storm of clouds and light forming in the middle. The loose rocks around the team began to shake and rise off the ground.

"It's creating a wormhole," the professor screamed. "It's going to suck everything in. There's nothing we can do! We've ran out of time!!"

Boulders and large sheets of ice were now flying skyward as the wormhole expanded even more. The people on the ground were trying to tether themselves to any rock that was secure but it was futile and one by one they began to lose their grip as the wormhole sucked them up screaming into the sky.

Charlie was still tethered to the life line and as he stared in horror at the carnage around him, his left hand slowly dropped to the firearm strapped to his hip.

"Our decisions will build our future," he said quietly.

His thumb and forefinger popped the guns holster clip.

"Our decisions will build our future." He said again slightly louder than before, competing with the howling wind and the screams of the doomed men.

He slid the gun slowly out of its holster. The firearm recognised his fingerprints and powered up.

"Our decisions will build our future!" he shouted.

The professor, intent on holding on to a nearby boulder looked across at Charlie as the boy slowly raised the gun.
"What the hell are you doing??" screamed the professor. "Charlie don't!"
Charlie smiled kindly at the professor.

"If I'm not here, then all this can't happen,

right?" he screamed.

"Time will repair itself. OUR

DECISIONS WILL BUILD OUR

FUTURE!!"

And with that, he put the barrel of

the gun into his mouth...

and pulled the trigger.

∞

*Lewis Davies*

# Epilogue

The sun was hot on his face and Charlie had difficulty opening his eyes. He could see the dim red of his eyelids blood vessels due to the excruciating brightness in front of them.

"Are you ok?" A muffled familiar voice seeped into his ears and Charlie very cautiously and slowly opened his eyes.

He squinted in the blinding sun until a shadow passed over his view and Jamie's face filled his vision.

"You ok mate?" Jamie asked again. "You took a nasty fall. Too busy watching those bloody birds rather than where you were going."

"What happened?" Charlie asked, a little dazed.

"You tripped over that rock and smacked your head off that rock," replied Jamie pointing exaggeratedly to first one boulder, then another. There was a small blood stain on the latter.

"My head is killing me!" said Charlie, putting his hand to the left side of his brow and looking at the blood on his fingertips.

"Come on mate, we'd better get you to the hospital." What were you thinking of fella? You were away with the fairies. Probably thinking of Hannah."

"I, I don't really know what happened," Charlie replied. All I can remember was walking across there, then there seemed like a blinding flash, a rush of noise; wind, screaming, voices, I don't know. Then I woke up just now with you standing over me."

"Well, you took a stumble and a big knock to the head. Come on. Let's get you out of here".

As Jamie put his arm under Charlie's and started to help his friend to his feet, a small stone fell out of the top of Charlie's partially unbuttoned shirt and hung down on a gold chain.

"What's that then?" Asked Jamie.

Charlie took the pendant flat in his hand and stared at it. The stone was finely polished and was in the shape of a butterfly flapping its wings.

"Where did you get that?" Jamie asked. "Not seen you wearing that before."

"To be honest, I don't know." answered Charlie, looking confused. "It looks familiar though but I can't remember where from."

"Maybe you got it from Hannah?" teased Jamie, lighting another cigarette with his zippo. "So," he continued. "Are you gonna ask her out then?"

"Don't know," replied Charlie. "Maybe."

"It's not that big a decision," laughed Jamie.

"Our decisions will build our future," Charlie answered quietly.

And with that, the boys picked their way out of the quarry and disappeared across the fields.

*Lewis Davies*

A peregrine falcon lazily soared across the sky.

*The End?*

Printed in Great Britain
by Amazon